# Bury Me A G 5
## *The Prequel*

**Lock Down Publications
Presents
Bury Me A G 5
A Novel by *Tranay Adams***

Bury Me a G 5

**Lock Down Publications**

P.O. Box 870494

Mesquite, Tx 75149

Copyright 2015 by Tranay Adams Bury Me A G 5

First Edition September 2015
Printed in the United States of America

*This is a work of fiction. Names, characters, places, and incidents either are products of the author's imagination or are used fictitiously. Any similarity to actual events or locales or persons, living or dead, is entirely coincidental.*

**Lock Down Publications**
**Email:** tranayadams@gmail.com
**Facebook:** Tranay Adams
**Like our page on Facebook: Lock Down Publications**
@www.facebook.com/lockdownpublications.ldp
**Cover design and layout by:** Dynasty's Cover Me
**Book interior design by**: Shawn Walker

Tranay Adams

# CHAPTER ONE
## Los Angeles
## 1982

*Honk! Hoonkk! Hooonkkk!*

"Come on now, get the fuck outta the way!" Melvin screamed aloud, veins bulging at his temples and neck. He was doing seventy-five in a thirty-five mile an hour zone, dipping in and out of lanes, narrowly missing other vehicles. His heart rate was jacked and his adrenaline was pumping. He was on the clock, trying to get to the hospital because his wife, Kimberly, was in labor.

He was speeding so fast on the black top that the white lines on the streets as well as the stop lights looked like blurs to him. He snatched his eyes off the windshield and glanced at his watch. It was now 9 o'clock. Someone on the hospital staff had called him at work at 8:15 P.M to let him know that his wife was going into labor, which was forty-five minutes.

"Shit!" Melvin cursed, seeing the time. He was sure that his wife was well into the proceedings to give birth to their first child by now. Hopefully he was wrong, because he really wanted to be there in the room when his offspring was pushed out into the world. His head snapped back and forth between the windshield and the side view mirror, gripping the steering wheel. "Hold on, baby, you hold on! I'm almost there, just hang on!" He said to Kimberly as if she was there riding shotgun.

When Melvin looked into the side view mirror he saw a Toyota pickup truck speeding up along the right side of him. The pickup was going so fast that he was sure that the asshole driving it was trying to stall him from getting over into his lane, but he wasn't about to have that shit. Fuck naw!

"Nah, not tonight, homeboy, you got me fucked up!" He swerved into the lane just as the Toyota was coming up, nearly causing an accident. The driver of the pickup honked his horn with a vengeance and stuck his head out of the window, cursing his ass off.

"You stupid son of a bitch!" the man spat fire from between his thin pink lips, the lower half of his face covered by a bristly, dirty blonde beard. He stuck his meaty arm out of the window and held up his chubby middle finger, steadily leaning on his vehicle's horn.

*Honk! Honnnkk! Honnnkkkkk!*

"Suck my dick!" Melvin hurled back at the irate driver and held his middle finger out of the window as well. He didn't give a fuck about anyone else on the streets. He was trying to make it to the hospital in time to cut his newborn son's umbilical cord. "Aww, shit!" Melvin stated, seeing traffic ahead. Looking to his left, he saw a young man on a royal blue Huffy bike, standing up on its pedals, riding down the sidewalk. The youth was going so fast that the wind was blowing against him and ruffling his clothing.

*Fuck it,* Melvin thought to himself. He then drove upon the sidewalk and jumped out of his car, leaving the driver side door open. Running across the street, he came close to being hit by oncoming vehicles.

*Honk! Hoonnk! Hoooonnnk!*

The cars in the street blew their horns at Melvin and gave him a tongue lashing. He didn't pay them any mind as he made it upon the sidewalk where he saw the young man on the bike. He chased after him holding up a one hundred dollar bill.

"Yoooooo! Yooooo, stop! Hold up!" He called after him, face shining from sweat. The young man sat down on his bike and cruised. Hearing someone calling after him, he looked over his shoulder. Curious as to what the man holding up the money wanted, he mashed the brakes of his Huffy and skidded to a halt.

The young man stopped and twisted around, looking at Melvin with furrowed brows. He could tell he was exhausted and most likely parched.

"What's up?" the youngsta asked, throwing his head back.

"I'll give you a hundred dollas for that bike." Melvin held the dead white men out before the kid's eyes. He snatched the money from out of Melvin's hand and hopped off his bike, still holding on to the handle bar with one hand.

"Take it," the youngsta released the bike as Melvin mounted it, throwing his legs over it and sitting on the triangle shaped cushioned seat.

Melvin took off pedaling fast, flying up the block, wind ruffling his clothing. He went up and down slopes, zooming past people and making some dive out of his path.

"Fuck out the way, my wife's in labor!" Melvin bellowed while his face and arms were glistened from perspiration. He breathed heavily but he had to keep going if he wanted to be there for his family.

Melvin bounced up and down as he came down off a curb. His eyes were so tuned into what was ahead of him that he didn't even see the oncoming Pontiac Trans Am at the corner of his eye.

*Urrrk!*

*Bunk!*

Melvin flipped over the hood of the car and his bicycle fell to the ground on its handle bars. He was tired as a mothafucka, but he was determined to make it. As Melvin rose from the ground looking up at the Trans Am, he saw the driver's door open and an Asian lady stuck her head out. A concern look was plastered across her face.

"Oh my God, me so sorry, are you okay?" she asked timidly.

"I'm fine, lady." Melvin hopped up in a hurry and got on the bicycle, pedaling away. It wasn't long before Melvin found himself huffing and puffing. His sweat stained around his collar and his under arms a darker color. Reaching the underground parking complex of the hospital, Melvin jumped off his bike and let it fall to the ground. He took off running towards the elevator lobby. By the time he got to the elevator it was dinging and opening to head to the tenth floor, so he didn't even have to press the *up* button.

"Come on, come on, come on," Melvin impatiently tapped his foot and glanced at his watch again. It was an hour and twenty minutes since he'd last spoke to anyone at the hospital. His entire form was hot and glistening from perspiration. The beads of sweat that had formed on his forehead and the back of his neck ran like teardrops. He looked at each number as it lit up on the panel, waiting for the number seven to light up.

*Ding!*

As soon as the elevator's doors parted Melvin came sprinting out. He nearly fell but quickly regained his equilibrium, coming back upon his running feet again. Coming into the corridor, he breathed huskily and whipped his head from left to right. Remembering that his lady's room was on the East wing of the hospital, he ran down the right corridor. His head whipped from left to right looking at the numbers that was posted on the side of the respective doors aligning the hallway. The room number that he was looking for was, 762. He saw room 757, 758, 759 to his right, so he knew that room 762 was coming up soon. At that moment, the biggest smile stretched across his face. The date was here, the time was now. He was finally going get the chance to lay his eyes on his baby boy and the love of his life.

*Hold on, baby, I'm almost there,* Melvin thought to himself, hearing his thudding heart and labored breathing inside of his ears. Just then, a doctor emerged into the hallway from the room that he was headed to. He was in a surgical cap, a protect mask which he wore around his neck and scrubs that were speckled with blood. The man stopped when he looked down the hall and saw Melvin running in his direction. He wasn't for sure, but he had an idea who he was.

"Are you Melvin Petty?" the doctor asked curiously, once Melvin had stopped before him.

"Yes, yes, how you doing, doc?" Melvin shook his hand with both of his and tried to steal a glance into the room he'd just walked out of. "My boy make it here yet?" He asked with excitement. Homie was so anxious that he couldn't stop moving around.

A grim expression etched across the doctor's face and he looked away, shutting his eyelids and taking a deep breath. He then looked back to Melvin who looked concerned.

"Doc, is everything okay with my son?" Melvin asked worried.

"Yes, everything is okay with your son, but…"

"But what? What's the matter?" He tried to glance into the room again, hearing his son crying aloud. Hearing his offspring brought a slight smile to his face. He moved to enter the room, but the doctor placed his hand on his shoulder, stopping him.

"I'm afraid I have some bad news, Mr. Petty." the doctor finally told him.

"Yeah, what's up?" His brows furrowed.

At that moment, Melvin's heart began beating harder and faster in his chest. He swallowed the lump of nervousness in his throat and wiped away the sweat that threatened to drip from off his brows.

"Your wife," the doctor's eyes turned glassy and his nostrils flared. His bottom lip quivered because he hated to be the bearer of bad news. He already knew what he was about to lay on Melvin was going to crush him. Still, he had to tell him anyway. "Your wife passed away giving birth to your baby." He told him regretfully.

It was true. In Kimberly Leblanc Petty's final hour she pushed with all of her might, feeling an antagonizing pain like any other. An excruciating pain ripped through her stomach as she unknowingly started to hemorrhage, releasing her son into this cold world. As he took his first breath, she took her last.

Melvin's eyelids stretched wide open and he gasped. His mouth hung wide open as he held his hand to his chest and staggered backwards, looking like he'd been shot through the heart. Instantly, his eyes pooled with tears and his knees buckled. Still, he managed to stand. Feeling himself about to collapse, he staggered over to the nurse's station's desk. He grabbed hold of the edge of the desk, but eventually dropped to his knees. Tears cascaded down his cheeks and his hands trembled. He had become paralyzed by his hurt and devastation. It felt like all of his energy had been zapped out of him, and he had shortness of breath. He was gasping as if he had asthma. Dizziness invaded his mind and he saw double.

Melvin looked up and saw the doctor and some of the other staff member trying to help him to his feet. One of the nurses, and the doctor that had given him the bad news, managed to get him upon his feet. He buckled again, overwhelmed with grief. The doctor caught him and hugged him tightly. Melvin embraced the man tighter and threw his head back. His eyes were red webbed and spilling tears consistently.

"Nooooooo! God, oh God, why? I loved her, Lord, I loved her! She was the love of my life, my queen, my rib, my rock, my best friend…" Melvin sniffled and brought his head down, looking over the doctor's shoulder that was holding him. His red nose flared and his teardrops kept falling, staining the shoulder of the man's scrubs. "She's gone? Is…is she really gone, doc?" He asked as he held him at arm's length, staring into his face.

The doctor wiped his tearing eyes with the back of his hairy hand and nodded. Melvin's heart ached that much more getting the confirmation. At that moment, Melvin looked around. The entire East wing seemed to be silent. He was surrounded by hospital staff and a couple of patients. All of their eyes were tearing and watching him. They all felt his pain or couldn't imagine what he was feeling having lost his wife.

"I…I gotta be sure, I gotta see her," Melvin left the doctor where he was standing with him. He staggered down the corridor wiping his eyes. The doctor tried to grab him but he pulled away; he insistented on seeing his wife. "Kim! I'm coming, Kim! I'm coming, baby." He didn't know it, but two security guards and the doctor that was consoling him was jogging down the hallway after him.

Melvin reached Kimberly's room door and turned the knob, opening it. He had gotten it halfway open when he saw Kimberly's solemn face, eyelids shut and mouth forming a straight line. When the hospital staff that was still in the room saw him, they quickly covered her face with the sheet seeing how he was reacting. The wail of a baby brought Melvin's head around and he saw someone still dressed up to deliver babies holding who he knew was his baby boy. It was then he realized that he had lost one loved one, but had gained another.

Melvin was racked with grief. He couldn't stop the tears from falling, and his nose had gotten snotty from his sobbing. His form shivered and his legs felt like noodles under him. He moved to step inside of the room, but the doctor grabbed him from behind. He was too weak to fight him off so he allowed himself to fall back into him. The doctor lay with his arms around him and teardrops falling from his eyes.

Melvin stared up at the ceiling with tears seemingly pouring from out of his eyes and his bottom lip shaking. He tried to say something but the pain of the loss of his wife choked him up. He swallowed the lump of hurt that had manifested inside of his throat. He squeezed his eyelids shut and tears jetted down his cheeks. He made an ugly face feeling the emotional pain poisoning his heart. The man wanted to die right there on the spot so he could join his wife in heaven. But that was something that he couldn't do now that his son had entered this cold, heartless world. Nah, he had to be there in the flesh to groom his son for everything that would come at him on his way to adulthood.

\*\*\*

### An hour later

Melvin stood in front of the mirror inside the men's rest room, staring at his reflection. At twenty-three years old, he stood six foot two and had a dark caramel complexion. He had a thick goatee that outlined his mouth exceptionally. He had a wide nose and full lips. He had a slight muscular build and weighed a solid two-hundred and fifty pounds. Some would say that he resembled Ving Rhames, while others would beg to differ. It was safe to say that he was a fairly attractive man to most women, but at this very moment in his life, he looked a hot mess. Melvin's eyelids were so swollen from crying that they damn near were shut. His eyes were red webbed and his nose was also red. On his cheeks there were tears that had dried and now were white. Dried, green snot peeked out of his left nostril. If someone were to tell him that this was the worst day of his life, he wouldn't bother to argue with them.

Melvin unbuttoned his cuffs and shirt, removing it. He laid the shirt down on a nearby sink, leaving himself in his wife beater. The hairs of his chest showed through the collar of his wife beater and the few tattoos he had peeked out through the openings of it. After he turned on the dials of the faucet, he put a small pile of the pink soap into his palm from the dispenser. He lathered his hands and then his face, masking it completely white. Having taken the time out to stare at his self, he took a deep breath and broke down again.

Tears threatened to drip from his eyes and his mouth quivered. His shoulders rocked and he felt his knees buckling again. The thought of losing Kimberly fucked his psych up royally. His son would never have his mother and he would never have his wife...ever again. Realizing this, he knew he would have to come to grips and overcome the tragedy as best as he could. One of the hardest things that he would ever have to do was explain to his son that his mother had passed away when he came of age.

"Unh unh, nigga, suck that shit up! Suck it up," Melvin told himself as he gazed into the mirror. "You gotta pull yourself together, homeboy. Your prince is out there waiting to see his king, his father. You have to be everything that that boy needs in his life now that his mother is gone. You must implement strength and confidence each and every time you're in his presence, black man." He stated, holding either side of the porcelain sink. "Alright, okay. Okay." He looked down at the water swirling down inside of the drain. For a while he was silent, taking deep breaths. Afterwards, he rinsed the soap from his hands and then from off his face. He turned the dials to shut the water off and snatched several paper towels free from the dispenser. He patted his face dry and then dried off his hands. Balling the paper towel up, he tossed it over into the aluminum trashcan.

Melvin then put his shirt back on, buttoning up his sleeves and the front of it. Hunching over the sink, he gave himself the once over, turning his head from side to side. Although his face was clean of his tears, his eyes were still red webbed and slightly swollen. He wasn't back to his usual self yet, but his appearance would have to do for now. It was time that he met his baby boy; he didn't want to keep him waiting.

"Alright, Melvin, it's time you met your boy." He adjusted his leather belt and took a deep breath before leaving out of the men's restroom.

\*\*\*

Melvin stepped out of the men's room in time to find the nurse holding his son waiting for him. Seeing him in her peripherals, the nurse turned around to Melvin smiling. She had the baby cradled in her arms and he was wrapped snuggly in a blanket. As soon as Melvin seen the nurse and his child, a broad smile stretched across his face. Butterflies fluttered their wings inside of his stomach. The baby wore a blue beanie with *Like Father Like Son* emblazoned across it. Melvin wanted the beanie to be the first thing he wore when he entered the world.

When Melvin lost Kimberly he thought he'd never fall in love again, but he couldn't have been more wrong when he first laid eyes on his son. At that moment, he found himself head over heels all over again.

"Is that my lil' man?" Melvin asked, approaching and angling his head as he tried to get a better look at his son. He then opened his arms to receive him.

"It most definitely is," the nurse responded, passing him his child. "I'll give you two a minute." She touched his shoulder and walked away, smiling. She was so happy to see the baby's father so filled with joy, especially after losing his wife that night. Melvin turned his back to the nurse as she walked away. He had his baby boy in his arms and he was studying his face. The newborn had his mother's complexion, eyes and lips, but the rest of his features resembled the man cradling him in his arms.

"Heyyy, man, how you been, huh? How's daddy's lil' man been?" Melvin caressed his son's chin with the tip of his finger. A smile stretched across his lips and he kissed the newborn on his cheek. He then paced the hospital floor, coming back and forth across the window where you could see all of the lights of the city that night. The sight was one to marvel. It was unique, amazing, and remarkable. "Happy birthday, son, it's not gonna be easy, but I'm gonna show you how to navigate through this world. Our queen gave up her life so that you could live. That was the ultimate sacrifice. That right there proved a mother's love can't be matched." He became teary eyed thinking about the loss of his wife. He was a wreck and he didn't know how he was going to hold up, but he was definitely going to try to hang in there. "When I lost your mother I lost a huge part of me. That woman was the yin to my yang. I know now that I will never be right after her death. I can tell you now that I don't have much love to give, but what I have left in me, I promise to give it to you, son. All of it..." Melvin stopped and looked down into his baby boy's face; his eyelids were narrowed into slits and he looked sleepy as hell, but for some strange reason, the man believed that his baby boy heard and understood all that he said very well. "Losing your mother should only bring us closer together as a family. This should strengthen our bond as father and son. So let no one come between this union of ours, Tiaz." He smiled like a Cheshire cat. "You like that name, Tiaz? Huh, do you like it?"

He tickled baby Tiaz' chin and he slightly smiled at him. This caused Melvin to smile even further. "Well, Tiaz, your OG is glad you approve of your name. And as my son, I expect nothing short of greatness from you. You'll be a leader, a smart and intelligent man that oozes with confidence. Your actions will make an impact on people. They'll praise you. You'll do things in your life that'll guarantee that you'll never be forgotten. Your name will be on the minds and tongues of people forever. You'll be a legend for what you accomplish. Yes, sir, I can see it now, my baby boy, making folks remember his name...for a lifetime..."

# CHAPTER TWO
## 1997
### *Present*

"Haa! Haa! Haa! Haa! Haa!" Lavell bent the corner of the block running as fast as he could, shiny from perspiration. Sweat dripped from the corner of his brow and he had a frightened expression across his face. He tripped and fell, but quickly scrambled to his feet, running off in a hurry again. "Oh shit, oh shit, niggaz is tryna kill me!"

*Urrrrrk!*

The sound of tires squealing could be heard at the end of the block, where Lavell had bent the corner running from. Right after, there was a small white car that followed behind him; its driver had nearly lost control of the vehicle and crashed it. The vehicle was in a hurry to catch up with, you guessed it, that nigga Lavell. The car was in the background as the frightened man ran for his life, but it was hurriedly gaining ground on him.

*Blatatatatatatatatatat!*

A fifteen year old Tiaz hung half way out of the back window of the white car, which was a '93 Hyundai Elantra. He had a chrome Uzi .9mm pointed in Lavell's direction and was spitting hot fire at that ass. Tiaz' eyelids narrowed into slits as his automatic weapon jerked violently from its quick bursts of fire, sending empty shell casings flying everywhere. The young nigga wore a Houston Astros cap low over his brows and an orange bandana over the lower half of his face. The black sunglasses he had on concealed his eyes. There wasn't anyone on earth that knew who he was, short of God Almighty.

"You hit 'em yet? You hit 'em?" Threat asked from behind the wheel of the compact vehicle. He wore the same disguise as his comrade.

"Nah, I didn't get that bitch ass nigga." Tiaz announced to his main man. He then watched as Lavell continued his sprinting, seeing him near a gate of a vacant lot. The lot was full of tall dead grass the color of hay. "Nigga 'bouta hit the gate! Pull up and I'ma hop out; cut his black ass in half!" He settled back down in the seat and held on to the door's handle. He scowled as he waited for the right time to hop out and get busy with his tool.

"Alright," Threat mashed the gas pedal, building up speed in the Hyundai. The cars lined up on either side of the block looked like blurs the car was driving past them so fast.

*Urrrrrk!*

Threat slammed on the brakes and brought the compact vehicle to a skidding halt. As soon as the car ceased movement, Tiaz hopped out of the car with his Uzi held up at his shoulder. He was just in time to see Lavell landing on the other side of the gate on his bending knees, taking off running as fast as he could. Homeboy was moving so fast that Tiaz could see the bottom of his sneakers. The heels of his sneakers were hitting him in his rear end.

Tiaz ran over to the gate and took a look all around him. There wasn't any one in sight that could testify against him. Seeing that the coast was clear, he stuck the barrel of his Uzi through one of the openings of the gate. Closing one eye, he took aim and gripped the automatic weapon steadily. Tiaz' heart thudded inside of his chest and his adrenaline rushed the blood throughout his body. He wasn't nervous because he'd given a nigga the business before. Killing had become easy to him after he got the third tombstone under his belt.

Having lined up his weapon's sight with a fleeing Lavell's back, Tiaz took a deep breath and pulled the trigger back.

*Click!*

Tiaz' forehead crinkled and he looked at his Uzi. The goddamn thing had jammed up on him. *Fuck!* Looking up and seeing Lavell escaping, he tried to un-jam it as quickly as he could, but it wouldn't budge. Looking back up, he saw that his victim was far away and almost to the other gate on the opposite side. If he hit this gate then he would surely get away, and he couldn't have that shit. Nuh unh!

Tiaz went running back toward the Hyundai in a hurry, looking around again to guarantee that he wasn't being watched. He jumped back into the backseat and slammed the door shut behind him.

Threat took off, racing down the block as if he was in a high speed chase.

"What's up? Why you didn't pop that nigga?" Threat questioned him, looking back and forth between the rearview mirror at Tiaz and the windshield, as he sped down the residential street.

"This whack as Uzi jammed up on me, man. Don't wet it though, bro. He finna hit the next fence so he'll be on the next block. Punch out and catch up with his ass before he gets away." Tiaz informed him as he continued to try to un-jam the Uzi.

"I got chu faded." He gave him a nod and punched out, mashing the gas pedal further. The red hand on the speedometer swept around the circle. The Hyundai blew past the cars and houses aligning both sides of the block. The vehicle neared the right side of the street heading towards the corner.

*Urrrrrrrk!*

Threat made a tight turn that nearly flipped the Hyundai over, leaving it on three wheels for a second before it came back down on the black top. Threat mashed the brake pedal a little as he bent the corner of the next block. He mashed the gas pedal again and the red hand hastily made its way around the speedometer.

*Vroooooom!*
*Woop! Woop! Woop! Woop!*
The air surrounding the small car sounded as it went flying down the street. It past several cars and houses making them look like flashes of color on either side of the car.

Threat looked to the left side of the windshield and saw Lavell climbing over to the other side of the gate.

"He's coming up now!" He stated to Tiaz, glancing up at the rearview mirror. He reached between the console and the driver seat and pulled out a Glock .40. The handgun had an extended magazine, and it was as long as a measuring ruler.

"Alright, man, fuck it!" Tiaz sat the Uzi aside since he couldn't get the mothafucka to function. His gloved hand took a .9mm Beretta off his waistline. He cocked the bitch and scooted closer to the passenger door so that he could hop out once they were up on Lavell's monkey ass.

Lavell landed on his bending knees and looked to his right, seeing the Hyundai speeding towards him. He took off running, and before he knew it he was being stuck by his enemy's car. Upon impact, Lavell's L.A fitted cap went up into the air. He rolled over the hood of the car and crashed to the street. Wincing, he scrambled back upon his feet and kept on running. He would be in some hell of a pain once his adrenaline wore off, but that was the least of his concerns, his black ass was trying to stay alive.

In the background, Tiaz and Threat were hopping out of the Hyundai which they left parked in the middle of the street. They were on Lavell's heels as he made hurried foot steps towards a mini market/ apartment. His gold chains jumped up and down around his neck as he ran forward. His face and arms were glistening. His sweating had caused the wife beater he wore underneath his white T-shirt to be visible. He was exhausted, but there wasn't any way in hell he was stopping to catch his breath. To do so would be suicide with the two young thugs on his ass like stink on shit.

Lavell crossed the threshold into the store with Tiaz and Threat at his rear. He ran down the aisle throwing down racks of candy and potato chips to slow his pursuers down. "Lock the door behind you, my nigga, and hold it down! I'll get this punk ass nigga!" Tiaz jumped and hopped over the spilled racks of goods that were scattered over the floor. Behind him, Threat did like he said and turned the *Open* sign over to the *Closed* side. He then turned his gun on the clerk behind the counter. The terrified man threw his hands up in the air quickly, afraid of being shot down in his own store.

"Who else up in here?" Threat asked as he approached, keeping his gun pointed at his chest.

"No…no one." the man visibly trembled.

"If you lying, that's gone be yo' ass," he warned.

"I swear to God."

Meanwhile, Lavell kicked open a door at the back of the store and ran up a flight of steps. As he made his way up the staircase, all that could be seen was his silhouette and the lighting of the establishment shining at his back. Making it up the staircase to a chipped green apartment door upstairs, Lavell noticed that the door was cracked open. He shoved the door open and it banged off of the wall. Crossing the threshold, his head whipped from left to right looking for somewhere to run. When he looked to the window and saw the fire escape, he ran over to it and tried to pry it open.

"Ah, ah, ah, bitch nigga, not so fast," the menacing voice coming from behind Lavell froze him dead in his tracks. With his back to the apartment door, he slowly raised his hands up in the air. "There you go, girlfriend, now turn yo' mark ass around!" On his command, Lavell did just like he was told. Now that he was facing Tiaz, beads of sweat ran down his face and the back of his neck.

"Come on, youngsta, you ain't gotta do this. Whatever that nigga Cordell paying you, I'll double it...fuck it, I'll triple it. Just let me go, fam!"

"Nigga, you know damn well yo' pockets ain't as swoll' as Boss Dawg's. If they were you wouldn't be working for him in the first place."

Lavell had made the mistake of slinging his own work in place of Cordell's, the neighborhood dopeman, and the nigga he worked for. Cordell had been suspicious of the money he'd been getting recently from that particular spot. This was because he wasn't getting the normal amount of money that he usually gets from it. This was strange, very strange considering all of his other crack houses were doing the numbers that they were supposed to.

Coming to the conclusion that something was definitely up, Cordell sent a crackhead over to his spot to cop drugs. When he came back with what Lavell had given him, the gangsta compared the product to his own. He then had the junkie smoke the shit in front of him. He tried the rock that he'd copped off Lavell and then the rock that Cordell had for him. The crack he'd smoked that Lavell had served him had too much bacon soda on it while the one Cordell gave him was pure. This was because the crack king didn't put any cut on his product. He served his shit to the hood raw and uncut. It was from this, and through further investigation, that he confirmed that Lavell's trifling ass was on some shady shit.

"Mannnn, you must ain't know I..."

"Save it, fam," Tiaz told him from behind the trigger. At that moment, he heard hurried footsteps coming up the staircase loud and clear. He didn't even bother to turn around because he knew that it was his man, fifty grand, Threat.

Threat came to stand beside his homeboy with his gun out by his side.

"You straight, Crimey?" He looked from Tiaz to Lavell.

"Yeah, I'm straight. What chu do with ol' boy down there at the register?" Tiaz inquired, keeping his banga and his eyes on Lavell's scary ass. If homie made one move then he was going to send some hot shit flying at that ass.

"I locked the door down stairs and hog tied his ass. I also ripped the phone cord out of the wall to make sure he can't call nobody, even if he does get loose."

"My nigga," Tiaz chuckled. "That's why you my goon, you stay on the money. I fucks with chu."

"I fucks with you even harder. You know how we do," Threat dapped up his main man.

"Now, as for this fat faggot," Tiaz mad dogged Lavell. The imitating expression on his face made Lavell trembled. He looked up to the ceiling and made a silent prayer to God. "Boss Dawg wants us to make an example out of him."

"Then let's make an example, my nigga." Threat pointed his Glock at Lavell.

"Obliged," Tiaz tucked his Beretta at the small of his back and started in Lavell's direction, cracking the knuckles on both of his hands. He had a plan in mind, but he knew his bitch ass was going to buck against him when he set it in motion. This is why he had to beat that ass into submission.

Lavelle was as scared as a church house mouse when Tiaz walked up on him. His eyes were big and his bottom lip trembled, not knowing what he planned on doing to him. He was caught off guard when the young nigga punched him in the gut and knocked the wind out of him. When he doubled over, the young nigga punched him in the opposite side. He followed up with a punch on the chin that dropped his big ass on his hands and knees. Once he was there, Tiaz worked his ass over. He stomped, kicked and punched him. By the time he had finished, his forehead was sweaty and his knuckles were bloody.

"Help me grab this mothafucka, Crim." Tiaz scowled and grabbed Lavell by the back of his collar, dragging him towards the window. The man struggled to get loose as he thrashed his legs.

"What chu about to do with 'em?" Threat tucked his gun at the small of his back and advanced in his crime partner's direction.

"I'm finna toss his bitch ass off the roof," he replied. Hearing this, Lavell's eyelids snapped open and his heart thudded hard as fuck in his chest. He hollered out for help and thrashed his legs harder, but his efforts were useless. Whether he wanted to or not he was going to be thrown off the roof of the apartment.

Tiaz gritted his teeth as he tried to lift open the window. It took him three good tugs, but he finally managed to open it. Reaching down, he grabbed the back of Lavell's shirt and began pulling him up to his feet. Looking at his face he could see that his left eye was swollen shut and his nose was broken. He'd given the man quite the beating and was contemplating on giving him another one.

"Wait, man, wait…" Lavell pleaded.

"Mothafuck a wait, nigga, you pulled some punk shit, so now yo' ass gotta get dealt with." Tiaz grabbed Lavell by one arm and Threat grabbed him by the other. The man dropped his weight and made it harder for the young niggaz to carry him.

"Get up! Get cho punk ass up!" Threat ordered. When homeboy wouldn't move, he and Tiaz punched, stomped and kicked him until he was barely conscious and battered. Specs of his blood speckled the wall surrounding the window.

"Help me carry this fat fuck out on to the fire escape." Tiaz told Threat. They both grabbed two limbs each. Lavell was so out of it that his eyelids were narrowed into slits and his head bobbled about. He moaned in pain, unable to stop his pending fate.

"Got 'em," Threat said, having grasped their victim's arm and leg.

Tiaz and Threat carried Lavelle out of the fire escape and on to the roof of the apartment. The man was three-hundred and thirty-five pounds so they were sweaty and out of breath from lumbering him. Finally, they had made it to the ledge of the roof top.

"Alright, now, on the count of three, we're gonna toss his big ass over this mothafucka," Tiaz gritted his teeth, struggling to hold Lavell up.

"Got cha," Threat also gritted his teeth, beads of sweat sliding down his face. The sun was beaming brightly on all three of them, casting a rainbow through its florescent rays.

"Okay," Tiaz and Threat rocked Lavell back and forth as they prepared to toss him off the rooftop. "One, two…"

"Huh?" Lavell snapped awake, looking around with bulging eyes and a wide open mouth. Looking over his shoulder, he saw the streets below and the automobiles passing through them. He also saw the neighboring houses, power-lines, clouds and pigeons flying across the sky. He was afraid of heights, so the ground appeared further down than it was and he felt nauseated. "Wait! What the fuck are you doing?"

"Three!" Tiaz called out as he and his crime partner went to toss Lavell off the roof. Just as they released him, he grabbed Threat's jean's leg and held on for dear life. He was almost three times the young nigga'z size so his dead weight was dragging him toward the edge of the rooftop.

"Lemme go, bitch!" Threat clenched his jaws and kicked Lavell in the face repeatedly as he held on to him.

Lavell squeezed his eyelids shut and tried to turn his head, but the kicks came back to back.

"Aaahhhhh! Aaahhhh!" Lavelle hollered aloud, taking kicks to the face from Tiaz as well. He felt himself getting dizzy but he knew that if he let go then he was going to freefall.

"Let the homie go, let 'em go!" Tiaz kicked and kicked him as hard as he could. The son of a bitch wouldn't release Threat's jean's leg though. "Fuck this shit," Tiaz pulled out his Beretta and pointed it at Lavell's skull. When the big man saw the deadly end of the weapon pointed at him, his eyelids stretched wide open and he gasped. Instinctively, he let go of Threat's jean's leg and plummeted toward the streets below.

Lavell screamed at the top of his lungs. His mouth was stretched so wide open that you could see his cavities and his uvula, which was shaking from the intense volume of his voice. He flailed his meaty arms and kicked his legs wildly. The air from his fall rushed up from beneath him ruffling his shirt, causing his twin gold chains to float up in the air.

"Aaahhhhhhhh!"

Lavell's eyes looked like they were about to pop out of their sockets. He screamed so loud that he went hoarse. His heart dropped and his stomach turned as he stared down below. It looked like the street was flying up toward him fast.

*Poppp! Snappp! Crackkk! Snappp!*

Lavell's legs impacted the street and broke in halves. He lay on the black top, on his back, staring up at the power-line above him, tears dancing in his eyes. The sun shined down on the silhouettes of three pigeons sitting on the power-line. A second later, a fourth pigeon landed on the line.

"Ahhh, fuck, my legs, my fucking legs!" Lavell hollered out in excruciating pain. He lay awkwardly in the streets with his legs twisted at funny angles and their broken bones poking out of them. Meanwhile, Threat lay on his back on the rooftop of the apartment. He stared up into the sky breathing hard, and thankful that Lavell hadn't pulled him down with him. The young nigga lifted up his sunglasses and pulled his orange bandana down from around the lower half of his face. He did this so that he could breathe easier. A silhouette eclipsed him as he lay where he was on the rooftop. It was Tiaz. He outstretched his hand and pulled Threat to his feet. The young nigga dusted his self off and picked up his Glock, tucking it back on him.

"You okay, my nigga?" Tiaz asked with concern.

"I'm straight, Crimey. Good looking out." He dapped him up and gave him a gangsta hug.

Tiaz and Threat ran over to the edge of the rooftop and looked down below. They found Lavell lying in the street with his legs lying at funny angles underneath him. They could also hear him still hollering out in pain.

Hearing police sirens approaching from a distance, Tiaz nudged his partner in crime and they retreated from off the rooftop. Once they made it downstairs, they popped the trunk and dumped him inside of it. Slamming the trunk shut, Tiaz and Threat sped off down the street.

Tranay Adams

## CHAPTER THREE

Meanwhile, inside of the junkyard, Cordell stood outside of his luxury vehicle facing the entrance of the junkyard beside his enforcer, Savino. Cordell was wearing a pair of round lens sunglasses with gold frames and a silk white suit. He chewed on gum and pulled back the sleeve of his shirt to check the time on his Audemar.

Savino was a stocky cat of a caramel hue and slanted eyes that made him look like he was part Korean. He wore a white doo-rag with the flap and a Braves fitted cap on top of it and cocked to the side. He had on a wife beater which he wore beneath a matching Braves jersey. Lying on top of his wife beater were several icy platinum chains and on his right wrist he wore an iced out Cartier Tic Tac Toe watch.

Savino looked more like a rapper from the early 2000's era than the goon he really was. From his appearance you'd think that he'd most likely but a rhyme than a gat. Being that it was '97, his style of dress was ahead of his time, but he did fancy himself a trendsetter.

Cordell pulled a handkerchief from out of his back pocket and patted the beads of sweats from off his bald, shiny head. He then patted the back of his neck and underneath his chin as well. It was a scorching 88 degrees that day and the sun wasn't showing anyone mercy. Once he'd finished patting himself down, Cordell slid the handkerchief back inside his back pocket.

"We gone give 'em five more minutes and then we gone raise up out this bitch." Cordell told Savino without taking his eyes off the entrance of the junkyard.

"See, I told you, you shoulda let me handle Lavell's trifling ass." Savino responded.

"I couldn't send you. Your face is familiar to him. He woulda known something was up."

"Look, here they come now." Savino nodded to the entrance and Cordell looked up. They saw the Hyundai backing into the junkyard with Tiaz sitting on the trunk. The compact car didn't stop until it was five feet away from Cordell and Savino.

"You're late!" Cordell told Tiaz.

"My fault, but it was traffic, and we hadda be easy out there. You know how many charges we woulda been looking at should we have gotten caught with this mothafucka." Tiaz patted the trunk and jumped off the car. At that precise moment, everyone heard the muffled hollers of Lavell as well as his punching of the inside of the trunk.

"Lemme outta here, man! It's hot in here, dawg! I can't breathe! I can't breathe!"

Lavelle complained with panic in his voice, dying to be freed from his close quarters.

*Bunk! Bunk! Bunk!*

"Shut cho ass up, nigga! That's what chu get for pulling that hoe shit!" Savino roared from where he was standing beside Cordell.

"Stand back, Tiaz," Cordell approached the trunk. "Yo', Threat, pop the trunk on this mothafucka, man."

*Thunk!*

The trunk cracked open.

Cordell and Savino stood outside of the trunk. The enforcer's face was fixed with a scowl and his .9mm automatic was out at his side.

"Open this mothafucka up." Cordell told him.

Savino gripped his gun tighter and settled his itchy trigger finger on the trigger. He then lifted up the trunk. Inside they found a perspiring Lavell. He looked exhausted and in pain. Beads of sweat ran down his face and arms. There were sweat stains around the collar of his shirt and where his armpits were. His broken legs were twisted in opposite directions. Where he had been bleeding on the trunk's carpet had turned brown from his blood drying. The sun was shining on Savino and Cordell's backs, casting their shadows on Lavell.

When Lavell saw Cordell and Savino, his eyes got as big as saucers and he gasped like he'd seen ghosts. He looked from left to right. He was petrified.

"Cordell, Savino, lemme explain..."

"Fuck your explanation!" Cordell grabbed him by his gold chains and pulled them against his throat, trying to choke him to death. He pulled so tight that veins bulged at Lavell's temples and his eyeballs looked like they were about to pop out of their sockets. His tongue hung out of his mouth and his lips trembled. He tried to claw up Cordell's face, but he turned his face from left to right to avoid his scratching. A scowling Cordell gritted his teeth and pulled the chains even tighter around his victim's neck. A bead of sweat broke free down the side of Cordell's face and the chains slowly began to come apart. Finally, the chains snapped and what was left of them fell onto the ground. Afterwards, still pissed off, Cordell punched Lavell square in the face. By the time he'd grown tired of punching him, he was breathing huskily and his knuckles were bleeding. Lavell's head hung out of the trunk. His eyes were rolled to their whites and his nose was bleeding.

"Pussy ass nigga!"Cordell spat on Lavell and then wiped his bloody knuckles off on the barely conscious man's T-shirt. He then placed Lavell's head back inside of the trunk and slammed it shut. Turning around, he looked up high into the sky and found Savino sitting inside of the machine that operated the magnetic crane, "Threat, gone hop out the car, youngsta."

Threat obliged Cordell.

With the sway of his hand, Savino motioned for Cordell, Tiaz and Threat to clear the path for him to grab hold of the Hyundai. Once they were out of the way, he brought the magnet over the rooftop of the compact car. The car shook a little, which disturbed the pebbles on the ground it was parked on. Abruptly, the vehicle slammed into the magnet.

Savino switched up the levers inside of the machine and brought the automobile over to the car crusher. As the Hyundai was craned over to the car crusher, everyone could hear Lavell calling out for help and pummeling the inside of the trunk with his fists.

"Hellllp me! Somebody hellllp me pleeeaasee!" Lavell called out over and over again.

*Boom!*

Savino pressed the button that released the Hyundai inside of the car crusher. He then shut the machine he was operating off, grabbed his .9mm off the dashboard and climbed out of the machine. He made his way halfway down the bars that were made to climb up into the machine with and jumped down onto the ground. Tucking his gun at the front of his jeans, Savino strolled over to the car crusher and pressed the button that started the machine up. The machine squeaked and made other noises that old metal makes when it's moved.

"Hellllp me! Somebody hellllp me pleeeaasee!" Lavell called out again and pummeled the inside of the trunk furiously.

Silence filled the air once the car crusher was through making scrap metal out of the Hyundai. Savino held his middle finger up at the Hyundai as he walked over to stand beside Cordell.

"Job well done, gentlemen," Cordell congratulated Tiaz and Threat.

"That ain't 'bout nothing. Me and my nigga do this shit all day long. Ain't that right, Threat?" He dapped up his homeboy.

"You ain't never lied, homeboy." Threat spoke to his right-hand man, but his eyes were glued on Savino. The two were staring each other down.

Tiaz' forehead furrowed when he noticed this, but he didn't mention it. Threat and Savino never felt one another. They both thought that the other believed that he was the hardest nigga in the streets and wanted to prove him wrong. The problem was Cordell wasn't having any unnecessary beefs because that fucked up his money, which was drug money. If the streets were hot because of violence then that meant there was going to be police presence. And this meant that his people couldn't move his narcotics.

"Y'all niggaz chill with that shit, man." Cordell barked, seeing exactly what was transpiring between his enforcer and the young head busta. "Y'all wanna measure dicks then you do it on yo' own mothafucking time. Not mine." He spoke stern.

"Anytime you feel like you wanna come for the crown, I'll be right here waiting to oblige you, young blood." Savino tapped the .9mm that was tucked at the front of his jeans. His mad dog stare was locked on Threat and he couldn't wait to shut his eyes forever.

"You never know, homie, today might just be the day." Threat whipped out his gun.

"Get cho boy, Tiaz, for this shit goes left." Cordell warned the young nigga.

"You got me fucked up, old head. Tiaz is my brother, and I love 'em to death. But he don't hold the leash to this dog."

"So, what's up, rookie? You up for a game of death?" Savino cracked a sinister smile.

"Money over bullshit, always remember...money over bullshit." Tiaz said to Threat.

Threat nodded and licked his lips, keeping his murderous eyes on Savino. Moving to tuck his gun, he said, "I'ma let chu keep yo' life today, pops."

"Another time another place," Savino replied.

"Jesus, you two hot head mothafuckaz need anger management." Cordell shook his head and then turned to Tiaz. "Lemme give y'all yo' blessings so you can get outta here." He reached into his pocket and pulled out to fat ass wads of money secured by rubber bands. He tossed one to Tiaz and the other to Threat. They didn't even bother counting the money; they stuffed the wads inside of their pockets and turned to walk away. They took three steps before they were called back.

"'Sup?" Tiaz turned around and threw his head back.

"Gemme a tick or two, would ja?"

"Lemme see what this nigga wont. I'll be right back." Tiaz told Threat before he headed over to Cordell to see what was on his mind.

Cordell threw his arm over Tiaz' shoulders and took a walk with him. He stopped once he figured that they weren't within earshot of Savino and Threat.

"Now, I got word that some niggaz have been setting the streets on fire out here. Niggaz extorting and robbing everything in sight," he placed his fist to his mouth and cleared his throat. "A couple of niggaz I know crack houses got hit, but you know what I noticed? Outta all of these niggaz that's getting the blues, my shit has been left alone. So, I figured one or two things. These dudes that's running around out here sticking up shit just so happened to pass all of my spots up, or they just don't have balls big enough to take shit from me." He looked Tiaz dead in his eyes. It was from this that Tiaz acknowledged that Cordell knew him and Threat had been the two niggaz he was talking about. "Now me being the nigga that I am, knowing that if a mothafucka was to ever take so much as a fucking crumb from off my plate, what I'd do to him or his big head ass partner. I'd have to say that those two cats I'm talking about don't have the balls to bring any of that bullshit this way. I don't play that shit, straight up. Niggaz will end up like Lavell over there in that mothafucking car crusher. You feel me?"

"I gotta go, man. Was that all you wanted?" Tiaz asked. He didn't even bother dignifying that question with an answer. The way he saw it, he was better off getting on his way before guns were drawn again and he found himself in a Mexican standoff.

"Yeah, you can go, kid." Cordell smiled and patted him on the shoulder. He then watched as Tiaz joined up with Threat and they walked out of the junkyard. Savino came to stand beside Cordell. "Yeah, I wish you lil' fuckaz would call y'all selves robbing me. There would be hell to pay." He took the time to spark up a Black & Mild and blew out a cloud of smoke.

***

Tiaz watched Threat's back as he stood behind him. The little nigga used a Slim Jim as he tried to pop the lock on the driver's door of a gold '88 Celebrity.

"Nigga was flexing too, like I know niggaz ain't got balls big enough to steal from me." Tiaz mocked Cordell's voice. "You know, like niggaz are scared or something. Old head got us fucked up. He must don't know me and my ace will bring it to any nigga that wants it. We don't give a fuck who he is or who he might be connected to."

"For real for real," Threat said as he focused on the task at hand with his tongue hanging out the side of his mouth. He was listening to his homeboy and working the lock at the same time.

*Thunk!*

The door came unlocked and Threat opened it, allowing Tiaz inside first. He then stuck the Slim Jim between the console and the seat.

Next, he went about the task of hot wiring the old car.

"He must don't know I'ma crazy ass young nigga that don't give a fuck about shit except you, pops and the hood. Everything else after that can kiss my ass."

"I feel you on that, Crimey." Threat said as he tried to get the car to start. Before he knew it there were sparks from the colorful wires pinched between his fingers and the automobile was roaring to life. "That's what I'm talking about, baby." He smiled and dapped up Tiaz. He then picked up the worn black leather bag that had all of the tools in it that he needed to steal something or someone.

Threat grabbed another tool from out of the bag and tossed it into the backseat. He stuck the tool into the ignition and turned it. He then adjusted the rearview mirror, pressed his foot on the brake, and changed the gears. He glanced into the side view mirror to see if anyone was coming and then he pulled out.

# CHAPTER FOUR
## *That night*

"I'm sorry, but I gotta let chu go!" Ralph said from behind his desk. He was a slender dude that wore his hair in a tapered afro. He was wearing a black windbreaker and a purple shirt. Emblazoned on the breast of the shirt was Platinum Protection.

Lemme go for what?" Melvin's face twisted in a scowl. His eyes were red webbed and his eyes had black bags beneath them. There was also dried white stuff at the corner of his eyes and his mouth. He looked exhausted, and he was too. He'd been busting his ass working two jobs. He pushed a taxi cab during the day and worked security at the Staple Center at night. Homie did all of this to keep his bills paid and a roof over he and his son's head. Melvin didn't have time to do anything but work. By the time he was getting off one job it was time to go to the other. His sex life wasn't much to speak of either. I mean, sure he had a couple of one nightstands since Kimberly's passing, but that was pretty much it.

"Late, late, late, late," Ralph sang, throwing his head from left to right. He leaned back in his black leather executive office chair. "How many times did I have to tell you, Melvin?" He jabbed the desk top with his finger, emphasizing every word that rolled off of his tongue. "These white folks don't play with their safety. Hell, don't nobody play 'bout dat. Now, you 'pose to be at work 9 o'clock sharp every night, Monday thru Saturday. That's with the extra day you requested. You're late every night. You clocking in at nine thirty, sometimes later. You know how many calls I've gotten from the powers that be chewing my black ass out about chu? Huh? Do you know how many times I've lied just so you could keep yo' job?

I'm sure you don't. Even if I was to tell you, you still wouldn't believe me."

"Look, Ralph, I hadda getta second gig in order to make ends meet. I'm pulling ten and twelve hour shifts at my first gig and about ten here. That don't leave much of a window of time to get here, but I'm trying. I swear 'fore God I be breaking and shaking to get my ass down here for y'all, man."Melvin took a breath and gathered his wits. "Listen, man, shit been real hard for me, but I been trying to make it work. I can't under any circumstances lose this job. I got rent, life insurance, car insurance, medical bills, utilities, and most importantly, a son to take care of. If I lose this gig, there ain't no way in hell I can make it off what I'm clocking pushing that old cab of mine." Melvin ran both his hands down his face and continued, "I need this gig bad, Ralph, I'm asking you to please gemme one mo' chance. Whatever you gotta tell 'em people, please, tell 'em. I promise, on my wife's grave, this will be the last time ever I'm late for work. So, please, please, please, do whatever you can for me to keep this mothafucka, man." He begged with his hands together like he was praying.

Ralph stayed leaned back in his chair thinking as he massaged his chin. His eyes were focused on the portrait on his desk of his family. It was him, his wife, their three children and his newborn son. As bad as he wanted to stick his neck out there again for Melvin, he couldn't. His supervisor had been riding him hard for Melvin's repeated tardiness. The guy at The Staple Center that had taken out the contract with Platinum Protection had threatened to sever ties with the company if Melvin's tardiness continued, so this was the last draw for him.

Ralph's supervisor told him that the next time that Melvin was late that he had to fire him or he was going to fire his ass. There wasn't going to be any if's, and's or buts about it. He was going to see to it that Ralph was standing in the unemployment line. With a family to provide for, with the way that Ralph seen it, Melvin's ass had to go. That's just the way it was. Fuck it!

Ralph stopped massaging his chin and placed his hand on the armrest of his chair. He looked up at Melvin who had hope swimming in his eyes, wishing that he could give him the response that he wanted to hear.

"I'm sorry, Mel, but it's outta my hands," He held up both of his hands for emphasis.

"Come on now, Ralph, man," he looked at him like *You can't be serious.* "As far as we go back, I know you not gone do me like that, at least not atta time like this."

"Unfortunately, the well has run dry with chances. I've put my ass on the line far too many times already. By allowing you to stay here I'd be gambling with my family's future. That's not something I'm willing to put up at stake."

"My nigga, I know you can…" Melvin moved closer to the desk to address him, but he held up his hand, stopping him in his tracks.

"That's it, man. I'm sorry, but you gotta go." He pulled open his desk drawer and took out Melvin's last paycheck which was labeled with his name. He tossed it onto the desk top and it slid a little, stopping before him. "I'm gonna need you to hand over your windbreaker, shirt, badge and utility belt.

"Can't believe this shit, Ralph. This how you do your friends?" Melvin asked as he removed the stuff on him and placed it on the desk top. He'd taken off everything except his the purple shirt that made up his uniform.

"I need dat shirt, man." Ralph flexed his fingers, signaling for him to hand over his shirt also.

"Fuck you! I paid twenty dollars for this shirt, it came outta my check." He snatched the envelope from off the desk top.

"Ain't no need for name calling, let's handle this like civilized adults."

"Yeah, whatever, nigga," Melvin stashed his paycheck envelope inside of his back pocket and made his way to the door. Opening the door, he slammed it so hard that some of the accolades hanging on the office's wall fell.

As Melvin made his way across the parking lot, he ripped open the envelope and pulled out his check. He looked it over and discovered that he only had two-hundred dollars and fifty seven cents. This didn't surprise him since he had only gotten two days in. The money was little more than a drop in a pot of water when it came to going forth to paying for his bills.The first thing that came to his mind was copping himself an eight ball (three and a half grams of crack) and trying to flip the earnings he'd received, but he reasoned that he was too old to be standing out on the corner going hand to hand. With that in mind, Melvin quickly threw his dope boy aspirations out of the window. He'd have to figure out another way to come into some money. With the kind of money he needed, he knew that whatever he did was going to most definitely be illegal. There wasn't any job that he possessed the skills to work that was going to pay him the kind of loot he needed to tackle his financial burdens.

Melvin reached his car and unlocked the door, sliding in behind the wheel. Gripping the steering wheel, he took a deep breath and shut his eyelids. He was so hot that he was turning red around his ears and neck. A vein etched up on his temple and his clenched the steering wheel so tight that his knuckles shown through his hands. Suddenly, his eyelids snapped open and he pounded the steering wheel, brutally. He then punched the driver side window and the ceiling of his vehicle, furiously. Afterwards, he screamed and screamed until he found himself growing hoarse. Next, he pounded the steering wheel with his fist again, accidentally honking the horn during his fit. Falling back against the driver seat, he shut his eyelids and breathed heavily. His chest rose and fell rapidly as he took air into his lungs. Peeling his eyelids back open, he turned his head to the driver's window and saw a royal blue '76 Mustang with black racing stripes. The original rims and metals of the car gleamed right along with its impeccable paint joint. This astonishing vintage vehicle belonged to no other than, Ralph.

Melvin smiled fiendishly as a light bulb came on inside of his head. He popped the trunk of his automobile and threw open the door, making his way to the rear of his vehicle. Once he'd gotten there, he lifted the trunk and found a bag of golf clubs. They were all of different shapes and sizes. He pulled out the one with the biggest end and shut the trunk as he walked away from it. Heading over to Ralph's Mustang, he practiced swinging the golf club. Once he made it to his old supervisor's automobile, he walked around it to check it out. It was truly a beautiful machine, worthy of the showroom floor.

Melvin stopped at the side view mirror and lifted the golf club high above his head. He scowled and his nose scrunched up, thinking about how he'd lost his job. Taking a deep breath, his shoulders relaxed and he swung the gold club down with all his might. The club whistled through the air en route to the side view mirror. Seeing himself in the side view mirror, and thinking about what he was about to do, Melvin stopped his club two inches above the side view mirror. His chest jumped up and down, as he breathed huskily. He then took the club away from where he'd stopped it above the side view mirror and lowered it at his side.

*What the fuck are you doing, Melvin? Yo' black ass is out here like a scorned lover about to take your frustrations out on this man's car. It ain't his fault that he couldn't save yo' job again. He gave you chance after chance after chance. Well, now all of those chances are gone. You can't blame nobody for yo' fuck up's but cho damn self. Now climb yo' sorry ass back behind the wheel of your car and drive off. Get cho self a bottle of something to think things over 'cause you gone have to come up with a money scheme, and fast,* Melvin thought to himself as he walked back to his car. He tossed the golf club into the backseat and hopped in behind the wheel. Cranking that bad boy up, he glanced into the side view mirror and pulled out. Money was the only thing on his mind as he pulled out into the street and drove off.

## CHAPTER FIVE

Melvin pulled up outside of Charlsey's mini mart & liquor and killed the engine of his vehicle. He hopped out of his ride and stepped upon the sidewalk, making his way inside of the ghetto establishment. As soon as he crossed the threshold inside of the store, he found the clerk looking up at the television set mounted high up on the wall. His arms were folded across his chest and the tube had his full attention. *A Bronx Tale* was on.

"'Sup, man?" Melvin asked as he approached the counter.

"Hey, how are you?" the African American clerk glanced back, but the movie had his attention.

"I'm good, bruh. Listen, lemme getta bottle of that Hen Doggy Dog and a pack of Newports," he pulled the few dollars that he had on him out of his pocket.

"Is that it?" the clerk asked, without bothering to take his eyes off the screen.

Yea...you know what? I needa get my son some cereal. Y'all sell Fruity Pebbles here?"

"I don't know, my nigga. Just check aisle three, that's where all the cereal is."

"Got cha," Melvin said walking off toward aisle three, thinking, *Fuck they hired that nigga for? He don't do shit.* He shook his head. *That's why mothafuckaz don't like hiring black people.*

Melvin went down aisle three looking through the colorful rows of cereal that were upon the shelf. Stopping at the center, he looked closely and smiled. He found the last box of Fruity Pebbles. Picking up the box, he made to go down the aisle back towards the register, but stopped short. He snapped his fingers as he remembered that he didn't have any milk back at the house. As he started back in the opposite direction, unbeknownst to him, a nigga in a red hoodie and matching bandana over the lower half of his face entered the store. He had his hands inside the pockets of his hoodie. The clerk was so focused on the movie that he didn't even notice homeboy. Melvin went down the refrigerator aisle looking for the milk. Finding the item he was looking for, he opened the glass door and grabbed a half of a gallon of milk. At that point, he was taken off guard when he heard a deep, menacing voice, full of intimidation.

"Open up the drawer, hurry up, nigga!" red hoodie screamed on the clerk as he pointed the dusty black .44 Magnum revolver in his face.

"Alright, man, alright, just don't shoot me!" the clerk pleaded, sounding like a straight up bitch. He was trembling all over as he punched in the keys of the register, making it ching. The cash drawer shot open and he quickly collected all the dollar bills inside.

"I won't the change too, Blood, all of it!" red hoodie spat. His black leather gloved hand clenched his revolver tighter.

"Okay, okay, okay," the clerk grabbed a brown paper bag and dumped the contents of the cash drawer into it. He tried to pass the bag to the nigga that was sticking him up, but he declined.

"Fuck that! Gemme a pack of swishers, a bottle of Jack…"

Melvin ducked down low and went to the other aisle. Peering out from the corner, he saw the clerk drop all of the extra items into the brown bag that the robber demanded. Once the robber received the bag, he looked up at the clerk who had his hands up, palms showing. The nigga was shaking so bad that his knees was knocking.

"Here's a tip, get chu some bulletproof glass up. It'll stop niggaz like me from robbing you," he chuckled and then said, "Have a nice night."

*Boom!*

The blast from the robber's cannon threw the clerk back against the shelf of liquor and he fell to the floor. Several liquor bottles fell to the floor and exploded, littering the linoleum with their contents.

The robber fled the liquor store. A moment later, the squealing tires of a car filled the air.

*Screeeeech!*

*Vrooooom!*

Melvin rose to his feet and ran over to the counter. Stepping behind it, he saw the clerk crawling to his feet and pulling himself up.

"Yo', my man, you alright?" Melvin inquired, seeing homeboy bleeding at his shoulder.

"Ahhhh, fuuuck, man. Hell naw, I ain't alright. That mothafucka shot me," he snatched up the telephone to call 9-1-1.

When he saw the clerk picking up the telephone, Melvin knew that he was about to call the cops. He counted out what he thought he owed for the items and smacked it down on the counter top.

"My man, that's for the stuff I got here. I'm gone. I don't wanna be involved in this shit when The Ones show up."Melvin grabbed his bagged items and hurried out of the exit.

Right before Melvin crossed the threshold out of the liquor store, he heard a line from *A Bronx Tale.*

*"Sunny is right, dad. The working man is a sucker…"*

\*\*\*

Tiaz wandered inside of his bedroom and kicked the door closed. His bedroom was decorated like most teenaged young men from the hood. On the wall over his bed was a painting of The Westside Connection's first album cover, which was of Ice Cube, Mack 10 and WC, set against a black background. He had a twin bed with mix matched pillowcase, sheets and blanket. His "20 square box television set sat on his nightstand which was missing a drawer.

Tiaz stepped before the mirror of his dresser and pulled out his Beretta, placing it down upon his dresser. As he stared at his reflection, he pulled off his hoodie along with the undergarments he wore underneath it. He tossed the clothing into the hamper which was by the closet. Taking a deep breath, he looked himself over and took in all of his features.

Tiaz was pretty tall for his age, standing five foot eleven and weighing all of two-hundred and twenty pounds. He lifted weights so his body was chiseled. He had a muscular, vein riddled form that looked like it had been forged from diamond. Across his broad back was *Hoover* in Old English letters. A bandana was tattooed over his left shoulder. On his right peck the Holy Cross was inked with *R.I.P Kimberly Petty*, along with her birth and death date. On his rib cage were the faces of his father, mother and godfather. Lastly, on his neck, was *74 HCG*. The young nigga looked thugged out with all of his ink and his cornrows, which reached his back. He also had blackened lips from smoking weed.

Tiaz looked at his hands and took note that he was missing some knuckles and the one that were there were darker than the rest of his hand. This was from years of fighting. You see, Tiaz was an all around good fighter. He'd been throwing hands since before he knew how to crawl. The young nigga didn't turn down any fair ones. He'd catch a fade with anybody, it didn't matter to him. He was big on respect and demanded it from any and everybody he encountered.

Tiaz flexed his muscles and made his pecks jump, one at a time. Keeping up his body was just as important as keeping up his street credentials. He wanted to be the hardest nigga that their ever was and he was determined by any means to be just that. He was dedicated to building up his reputation, and he knew that meant putting in work and showing mothafuckaz that he wasn't to be played with. This was why he made it his business to act a goddamn fool over even the smallest of violations. He wasn't taking any bullshit from anybody. He didn't give a fuck who they were or who they were related to. As far as he was concerned, anybody could get it behind his. Straight up!

Niggaz from his hood swore before God that he was crazy from all his criminal exploits. He was wilding out in the streets doing stupid shit and taking unnecessary risks. The young nigga knew that he wasn't quite right upstairs. He believed that all of his actions stemmed from the loss of his mother. A woman whom he had never met, but he knew he loved.

Time and time again, growing up, Tiaz questioned his father about why God had taken his mother away. At the tender age of five he believed that it was something he had done that made the Almighty deprive him of a relationship with his mother. Countless nights he cried himself to sleep wishing to be reunited with the woman that had given birth to him.

*A five year old Tiaz, who was dressed in Spider Man pajamas, stood in a chair. He was brushing his teeth as he stared at his reflection in the medicine cabinet's mirror. Foam from the toothpaste surrounded his mouth and specks of it clung to the mirror, with each stroke of his brush. Once he had finished, he turned on the faucet and climbed down from the chair. He washed off his toothbrush and rinsed out his mouth. Done, he dropped the toothbrush into the holder above the porcelain sink and wiped his mouth off on a towel on the rack.*

*"You finish, champ?" Melvin asked from where he was leant up against the doorway with his arms folded across his chest.*

*"Yep," Tiaz smiled.*

*"Come on then, big man." He smacked his hands and opened his arms to receive Tiaz. Tiaz ran over and jumped into his father's arms. He winced, feeling the weight of his son in his embrace. "Wow, you getting big, man. I nearly threw out my back."*

*"You getting old, dad."*

*"Yeah, I'm too old to be carrying your butt." Melvin cracked a grin and so did his son. He took the boy inside of his bedroom and laid him down in bed. Afterwards, he turned on the lamp light and tucked him in. He caressed his offspring's forehead with his thumb and then kissed him on the nose. "Goodnight, junior."*

*"Goodnight, dad, I love you so much."*

*"Right back at cha," He turned off the lamp light and walked out of the bedroom, pulling the door shut behind him.*

*Once he saw that his father was gone, Tiaz threw the covers from off him and climbed out of bed. Getting down on his knees at his bed, he put his hands together in prayer and shut his eyelids, saying, "Dear, God, I don't know what I did for you to take my momma from me. I don't remember if I was bad or not, but if I was, God, I'm sorry. I'm really, really sorry, God. I just…I just want a momma like the rest of the kids at school. I want a mom to gemme hugs, kisses, bake me things, tuck me in at night and read bedtime stories to me before bed. I have a father, and I am grateful for him, but I want a mom, too. I want to have both. I want a complete family, like Mykhal who sits next to me in Mrs. Squires class. He has a mom, a dad, a big brother and a lil' sister... a great, big family. Well, I don't need all of that, I just want a mom...my mom...please. Amen."* Tears slid down Tiaz' cheeks and he wiped them away with the back of his hand. He then crawled into bed and drew the covers back ove him. Unbeknownst to him, Melvin was standing outside his bedroom door with his back against the wall listening in. He shut his eyelids and tears jetted down his cheeks. Sniffling, he wiped his dripping eyes and licked his lips, continuing his way down the corridor towards his bedroom.

Looking to the corner of his dresser's mirror, Tiaz saw a photo of his mother wedged there. He plucked the picture from where it was tucked and stared at it. He admired his mother's beauty and her dazzling smile. Tiaz kissed the picture and exasperated as he longed to be with the woman that held him in her womb. He couldn't wait until the day came where he could hug and kiss her. The mere thought of it brought tears to his eyes and he took a deep breath.

Tiaz wiped his dripping eyes with the back of his fist and sniffled. He then opened his bedroom door and headed out, shutting the door behind him.

Tranay Adams

## CHAPTER SIX

Melvin lay stretched at the head of his head with his pillows propped up against his head and his fingers interlocked on his stomach. He was wearing a wife beater and black basketball shorts with his bare feet crossing one another. The television's screen's blue light flashed across his face. He wasn't paying attention to the show that was on though. Nah, he was thinking about the robbery that had taken place back at the liquor store.

His mind was like a VCR replaying the robbery over and over again. It all happened so fast. Homeboy in the red hoodie just walked up and pulled out that thang, demanding the money in the register. That particular liquor store usually stayed packed with patrons, which meant an okay amount of money went through the establishment. This led Melvin to believe that old boy that had stuck up the place had to at least get away with a few hundred dollars. Sure, it was easy money, but it wasn't enough to risk the time he would have gotten if he had been caught for the caper. Still, the nigga made off with a few hundred dollars in less than five minutes.

*Shiiiiit, I woulda never robbed no liquor store for them few lil' punk ass dollars and risk all of that mothafucking time. If homie would have been smart he woulda hitta bigger spot. That way he coulda made off with a bigger bag. Matter of fact, I would never hit any legal businesses, they most def' gone call the police. A nigga like me woulda hit some spots where they can't pick up the jack and call them people. A nigga like me woulda stuck up some drug dealers or some crack spots...wait a minute,* Melvin quickly sat up in bed as a light bulb came on inside of his head. He snapped his fingers and an enthused expression crossed his face. *That's what I'ma do to get this money to put me back on my feet. I'ma rob these niggaz in the dope game. Yeah, that's it! I mean, fuck they gone do? Call them folks and tell 'em a nigga hit 'em for they drugs and money? Fuck no! It's on now!* Melvin rubbed his hands together and smiled sinisterly.

*Knock! Knock! Knock! Knock!*

"Come in!" Melvin called out.

*Knock! Knock! Knock! Knock!*

Figuring that Tiaz couldn't hear him, he picked up the remote control and turned down the volume on the television.

"Come on in, son!" He called out again and sat the remote down on the nightstand.

Tiaz came through the door holding a picture of his mother. His father could tell that he'd been crying from his glassy eyes, but he didn't dare mention it. His son was a young man that made it his business to maintain a hardcore image at all times. Now, he didn't have a problem with telling his old man that he loved him, but he did have a problem with him seeing him shed tears.

To him, the only reason for a man to cry was if he'd just lost a loved one. As far as he was concerned his mother didn't count since she'd been dead before he'd gotten the chance to know her.

"What's up, son?" Melvin asked.

"Were you asleep, pop?"

"Nah, I'm wide awake, what's good?"

"I just wanted you to see something." Tiaz flipped on the light switch and sat on his father's bed, showing him the picture of his mother. She was a high-yellow woman with long eyelashes, rosy cheeks and a big smile. Her hair was done in individual braids and tied off at the end by a length of gold twine. She was absolutely stunning when it came to looks. It was safe to say that she was traditionally attractive.

"Wow, I remember this photo," Melvin smiled and took the picture from his son, staring at the face of his late wife, Kimberly Petty. "I took this one myself. I'd bought the camera offa smoker from around the way. I paid twenty bucks for that camera. It was a good one, too, straight outta the box. Me and your mother went up to the Santa Monica Pier. Boy, did she look beautiful coming outta that water in that bathing suit, glistening wet with the sun kissing off that flawless skin of hers." He passed the picture back to Tiaz. The young nigga looked down at the picture smiling, visualizing his mother running on the beach. He then saw her posing for his father to snap pictures of her. "'Til this day no one can convince me that your mother isn't, hands down, the most beautiful woman that I have ever laid eyes on. I just knew I had to have her. I wanted her to bare my children and I wanted to give her my last name. If I wasn't sure about anything in this life, I was sure that I wanted to put a ring on that woman's finger. If your godfather were here he could attest to that. Mannnn, me and your mother were in love. I didn't know happiness until she said yes to my proposal and I found out she was pregnant with you." He placed his hand on Tiaz' shoulder and gripped it. A tear dropped from Tiaz' eye and he quickly wiped it away, thinking of the love his mother and father shared. He wished more than ever that she was there with them. "I thought to myself finally, finally I'm going to have myself a family to call my own again." Melvin stared ahead smiling, looking like he was under someone's hypnosis.

"You ever miss her, pop?" Tiaz asked.

"Miss her? Mannn, my heart hurts each and every day I don't get to see that woman. Your mother was my soul mate, son. God made her for me and me for her. I don't have any doubts about that."

"I wish I had gotten a chance to meet her."

"I do, too. One day we'll all be reunited though. That's something I can promise you." He patted him on his back and gave him a half smile. Seeing that his son was feeling down about his mother, Melvin decided to tell him a story about him and his mother. "Hey, I ever tell you the story of how me and your mother met?"

"Nah, you never told me that story."

"Well, do you wanna hear it?"

"Hell yeah."

"I met your mother at The Bar Fly. This popular lil' dive over on the lower Eastside. I tried hollering at her, but she shot me down. She told me she was just there sulking over a recent breakup over a bottle of beer, so I left her alone. Later on that night, a knucklehead approached her by the name of Gamble. He tried to get her digits, but she told him the same thang she told me. Only this fucking cave man wasn't taking no for an answer. Anyway, he and your mother got into it. And I stepped in…so did the niggaz that were with him. I didn't give a fuck though. You know yo' old man, I ain't scared of nobody. I told that cock sucka I'd take 'em there and anywhere else if he wanted some, so…."

*"Step aside," Gamble pulled off his T-shirt and stepped up, accepting Melvin's challenge.*

*Melvin slid his foot forward, getting into a fighting stance. He thumbed his nose and lifted his fists, seeing his scarred knuckles before his eyes. He had the eye of the tiger and he was ready for whatever Gamble and his niggaz brought his way.*

*"Aahhhh!" Gamble rushed Melvin throwing haymakers, trying to knock his head off. Melvin swiftly dodged his advances and unleashed a flurry of punches on his torso. His fists were thrown so fast that they looked like blurs while en route.*

*"Ugh! Huuu! Uhh!" Gamble's eyes bulged and he doubled over from the impact of each punch. He tried to*

counter, but Melvin was on him like stink on shit. When Gamble swung on Melvin, he ducked and fired on his stomach with all of his might. The force behind the blow made Gamble vomit all over his wife beater before falling to the floor. He lay on the floor breathing heavily with food residue surrounding his mouth. Looking up, Melvin clocked DeWitt and Marlon charging at him. Whipping around in a 360 degree turn, Melvin slammed the heel of his sneaker into Marlon's jaw and broke it. The sound of bone breaking was heard by all of the patrons standing by watching the brawl. Marlon hit the floor hard and fast. He struggled to get upon his feet but the blow had left him weakened and hurt.

With Marlon out of the fight, Melvin set his sights on DeWitt. The bald head, muscle bound DeWitt proved to be more skilled with his hands than the others. He was able to land two solid punches to Melvin, busting his lip.

"Unh huh, you fucked around and got the right one tonight, mothafucka!"

DeWitt hit Melvin with two body shots and followed up with a hook. Melvin was quick on his feet though. He ducked the hook and followed up with three teeth rattling blows. Each punch that landed split DeWitt's lips more and more. Speckles of his blood clung to Melvin's shirt, but he didn't seem to notice. He faked like he was about to jab DeWitt and kicked him in the leg, where the bones connected instead.

"Arrrrrgh!" DeWitt threw his head back and hollered out in excruciation with his eyelids squeezed shut. Melvin then threw an overhand right that sent a ripple through his cheek and made his ear look like it was going to fly from off the side of his face. The assault dropped DeWitt to his hands and knees. He looked down at the surface and saw that he was bleeding at his grill, dripping blood all over the floor.

*"Come on, get cho bitch ass up!" Melvin motioned for him to get up with both his hands. If he didn't know how to do anything else it was fight. He'd been throwing hands all of his life. Hell, he had to. He was original from Alabama and he went to an all white school. Nearly everyone there was racist as shit. Back then, in the tenth grade, he was dating a white girl, so he'd get jumped often on the way to and from school which was a twenty mile walk.*

*One day, a couple of Caucasian knuckleheads gave him that work. Old Melvin ended up with fractured ribs and a broken eye socket. He did home study for the duration of school. Once he healed he hit the dojo hard for six months straight. He learned Chinese Kick Boxing. The next time he ran into those fools that beat him down, he made short work of them. That's right! He put all of their asses in the ICU. After that, their racist parents and the town's police had it out bad for him, so his parents sent him out to Southern California to live with Aunt and Uncle.*

*"Come on, get cho punk ass up!" Melvin egged him on. Seeing DeWitt trying to get back upon his feet, he gave him some space and threw up his bloody fists, looking for more.*

*"You're dead, you're dead!" DeWitt pulled himself to his good leg by grabbing hold of the pool table. Finally standing upward, he hobbled on his good leg and touched his mouth. When he looked to his finger tips they were bloody. Seeing this enraged him, so he snatched a pool stick from off the pool table. He did fancy moves with it, spinning it from the front of him to around his back so fast that it looked like a blur. "Yeah, yeah, come get some, bitch!" He tried to jab Melvin hard with the stick, but he dodged it. Before he knew it, the pool stick was being swung at his head multiple times. It made a swoop sound each time it was swung at him, but he was able to avoid contact.*

*When Melvin came back up from the stick being swung at his head, he kicked DeWitt square in the chest. The force behind the blow sent him high into the air. He landed down hard upon the pool table and sent some of the balls clattering into each other, eventually falling into some of the pockets.*

*"Oh my God, he's gotta gun!" One of the patron's called out.*

*"Look out!" Another patron shouted.*

*"Mellllviiiin!" Kimberly called out to him.*

*A wide eyed Melvin whipped around with his mouth hanging open. His eyes met Gamble who had just pointed his nickel plated .32. The small weapon gleamed beneath the illumination of the light coming from the ceiling. Before Melvin could react, Gamble was pulling the trigger and his gun was firing.*

*"Ugh!" Melvin's head whipped around and he went down in what appeared like slow motion to anyone watching.*

*"Nooooooo!" Kimberly called out with tears spilling down her cheeks. She ran over to attend to a wounded Melvin.*

*"Freeze!" a police officer commanded from behind Gamble. He whipped around to take a shot at him, but he cut loose on his ass.*

*The patrons cried out and cringed seeing the cop gun down the hoodlum.*

*Splocka! Splocka! Splocka! Splocka! Splocka!*

*Gamble winced as the bullets went through his body and splattered his blood on everything and everyone near him. He fired his .32 into the ceiling involuntarily before collapsing to the floor dead, losing his weapon.*

*"Please, God, don't let him be dead." Kimberly spoke to the Almighty. She then pulled Melvin over onto his back. When she laid eyes on him he had a nasty, bleeding gash*

*on his temple where the bullet had nicked him. Melvin stared up at her smiling and wincing at the same time from his wound. "You're alive, thank goodness." She kissed Melvin's affectionately. One kiss turned into two and then into three. Before she knew it they were kissing long, deep, hard and passionately. Turning their heads counter clock wise as they French kissed.*

*"So, I guess this means you'll go out with me?" Melvin smiled.*

*"No. It means I'm really thankful and I'll think about it," She smiled back at him.*

*"Do I gotta get nicked by another bullet to convince you?"*

*They laughed aloud.*

"...And the rest is history." Melvin finished telling the story.

"Pop, why you lying? You know them niggaz whooped yo' ass." Tiaz chuckled.

"Boy, you better ask someboy. Hell, I'm the one that taught cho young ass how to throw these hands." Melvin shadow boxed and showed off his footwork. You could tell by his movements that he knew how to fight well.

"Yeah, whatever, old man," Tiaz waved him off.

"What?" He threw some playful punches at his son and they started horsing around. They laughed and giggled as they wrestled around the bedroom. Later, they found themselves on the floor staring up at the ceiling.

"We're gonna be okay, son," Melvin told Tiaz. "We've just gotta hang in there."

"I know, OG. We will. It's me and you now; us against the world."

## CHAPTER SEVEN
### *The next day*

Melvin came waltzing out of the corner liquor store. He had a chocolate Zinger in his mouth and a carton of milk in his hand, which a scratch-off was placed against. The carton was propped against his stomach as he stared down at the scratch-off he had pressed against it, scratching off the boxes with a quarter. He was heading to his taxi cab barely paying attention to his surroundings. In fact, he never looked up from his scratch-off as he was walking, but he was still able to make it to his vehicle without incident and open the driver's door. He hopped in behind the wheel and slammed the door shut, sitting the milk carton aside on the passenger seat. He placed his scratch-off against the car's horn and leaned forth to finish scratching out the boxes of the yellow rectangle shaped card. The game was Ace's High and you had to scratch at least one number in the boxes that matched the number in the header above.

Seeing that he didn't win, Melvin threw the coin into the change tray and ripped the scratch-off into threads, tossing it out of the window.

"I don't know why I keep buying those goddamn things. I don't ever win shit anyway," Melvin cracked open his carton of milk and took a bite of his Zinger. When he was about done munching on his Zinger, he took a drink of milk and finished munching it down. Hearing someone outside of his window, he looked out of it and saw a crackhead with nappy, beaded hair. He was in a trench coat and beat up Rebocs. His sneakers were two sizes too big, so he had them laced up so tight that they curled at their ends. At that moment, he was standing before two niggaz. One was wearing a doo-rag and the other a NY fitted cap. They were looking at something that the crackhead was wearing as he held open his trench coat. As the crackhead held open his trench coat, he kept an eye out for the police. Melvin believed that this was because he had something illegal that he was trying to get the hoodlums to purchase.

"Alright, I give you thirty for it," the nigga in the fitted cap said.

"Thirty dollas, mannnnn, come on now. That's a crackhead price, shoot me at least fifty." the crackhead responded, scratching underneath his chin.

"Nigga, youz a mothafuckin' crackhead, what chu expect? Talkin' 'bout I'm givin' you crackhead prices. Look, check it out, either take the thirty for the vest or beat the street," fitted cap told him straight up.

"Awww, man, you can at least…" his words died in his throat as he put his hands up with his palms showing. He didn't want any problems once homeboy lifted his shirt and showed him his handgun, which was tucked inside the front of his sagging jeans, against his boxers.

"Aye, man, I don't won't no problems, chief!" The crackhead's voice trembled and his hands shook.

"I know you don't won't no problems, now get cho fonky ass up outta here 'fore I rob you!" He shoved the smoker fool and kicked him in his ass, lurching him forward and causing him to stumble. The nigga in the doo-rag busted up laughing with his hand on his stomach. He got a real kick out of the fiend's humiliation.

Seeing the crackhead take off down the street, Melvin finished off his Zinger and washed it down with some milk. He then closed the carton and sat it down on the passenger side's floor. He cranked up his vehicle and pulled out, busting a U-turn in the middle of the street. He drove alongside the crackhead as he ran down the block, tying up his trench coat and occasionally glancing over his shoulder. His eyes were full of fright and his mouth was wide open as he took in gulps of air. His face was shiny and beads of sweat had formed on his forehead.

"Yoooo, my man! My man, over here!" Melvin called out to the fleeing crack fiend. The scared man's head snapped in his direction and his forehead creased with worry lines. He mouthed *Oh, shit* and ran faster, thinking the hood nigga down the block had sent someone to get at him. His adrenaline was jacked up and he was afraid, so he never thought it was just a cab driver trying to get his attention. "Fuck, this nigga scared." Melvin said to no one in particular. He drove after the crackhead as he ran and fished around inside of his pocket. He pulled out his hand spilling loose change and wrinkled bills. Looking back and forth between the crackhead and the windshield, he dumped the contents from his pocket into the passenger seat. Still keeping his eyes on the windshield and the crackhead, he sifted through the wrinkled bills on the passenger seat until he found a fifty dollar bill. Holding it up so that the crackhead could see it, he called after him, saying, "Yo', my man, I need to holla at chu! Can we talk business? Huh? I wanna buy that vest from off you, homie!"

Hearing Melvin calling after him, the crackhead looked his way and saw the money. What the man said finally registered in his brain and he slowed down to a trot, eventually stopping. He bent over with his hands on his knees, hunched over and breathing hard, staring up at the man with the fifty dollar bill in his hand. By this time Melvin stopped his taxi cab in the middle of the street.

"It's...it's fifty dollas," the smoker fool told him, panting out of breath.

"I got it, fifty bucks, it's right here, homie." Melvin said, wagging the fifty dollar bill before his eyes. He then looked through the windshield and back window, seeing that there were cars coming and he was going to end up holding up traffic. "Check it out though; let's handle business in that alley over there," he nodded to an alley across the way. "I ain't tryna be caught up with the police 'cause I'm holding up traffic, tryna make an illegal sell. You feel me?"

"Oh…okay," the crackhead nodded and followed the yellow cab as it was driven inside of the alley. As he was approaching, Melvin had stopped the vehicle and hopped out, slamming the door shut behind him. The crackhead noticed he had a carton of milk in his hand.

"What's up, man? You look like you could use a drink." Melvin gave him the carton of milk. He watched as the crack fiend turned the carton up, drinking from it. His throat rolled up and down his neck. The white liquid spilled down his chin and neck. Once the crackhead finished drinking, he took the carton down from his lips and wiped his mouth with the back of his dirty hand. He tried to pass the carton back to Melvin and he declined it. With that, the crack fiend sat the milk carton on top of the roof of the cab.

"Alright, homie, lemme see the merchandise," Melvin rubbed his hands together in anticipation of seeing the bulletproof vest, hoping that it was authentic.

The smoker fool looked around cautiously as he untied his trench coat. Once he was sure that the coast was clear, he held his trench coat open and showcased his bulletproof vest, which had *Police* emblazoned across its chest. Melvin stepped closer to the crackhead and knocked on the vest. He then removed one of the plates from out of it and tested its weight. He also saw how thick the plate was. After he was done examining it, he placed the plate back inside of the vest.

"Sold," Melvin held up the fifty dollar bill. The crackhead snatched the wrinkled bill from out of his hand and removed his trench coat. He followed Melvin to the back of the cab, checking his surroundings as he waited for him to pop the trunk. Once he did, he unstrapped the vest and handed it to him. Melvin placed the vest inside of the compartment where the spare tire was hidden. He then slammed the trunk shut. When he turned around he found the smoker fool holding the bill he'd given him up to the sun light. He had one eye shut as he studied the currency for authenticity. Satisfied, he folded the bill up and slid it inside of his pocket.

"Pleasure doing business witchu," Melvin extended his hand and he shook it firmly.

"Look, G, if you need anything else, just lemme know. Now, I don't have a cell phone, but there's an old phone booth by my way that I can give you the number to should you need my services again."

"You could probably help me out with something now. You think you could get cho hands on a piece of iron for me?"

"Iron? You mean a gun?" He made his hand into the shape of a gun.

"Yeah, a gun," Melvin nodded. "Something clean…no bodies. Should I get caught with the mothafucka I'm not tryna sit down for a couple of years on the account of someone else's dirt. You follow me?"

"I got cha," the crackhead massaged his chin as he thought on it for a second. "Yeah, I can get chu a clean piece. No problem. Meet me back here, later on tonight…around eight o'clock."

"Alright, eight o'clock tonight, I'll be here; you just make sure you are."

"Oh, I most definitely will be there. I love crack, she's my bitch. And the only way I'm gonna get more of her is if I get my hands on the almighty dolla. Now, like I said, 'be here eight o'clock sharp'. I'll have your merchandise."

"You got it, boss. What's your name," he extended his hand.

"Jerome," he gave him a firm handshake and smiled, showcasing all gums where teeth should have been on the top row of his mouth.

"Melvin," Melvin cracked a halfhearted smile, seeing the smoker fool's fucked up grill.

\*\*\*

### Later that night

Melvin spent the rest of the day picking up and dropping off folks until 7:30 P.M came around. Seeing what time it was, he made his way back to the alley where he was suppose to meet crackhead Jerome. He parked at the end of the alley, leaving the nose of his vehicle sticking out in the alley's pathway so that he could keep an eye on it. The neighborhood he was in was notorious for having cars broken into and/or stolen and he wasn't trying to become a statistic.

Melvin made his way down the alley with a White Sox baseball cap pulled low over his brows and a jean jacket with the collar flipped up. His hands were inside of his jacket's pockets. The occasional gust of wind caused the collar of his jacket to smack up against his chin. Reaching the center of the alley, he pulled back the sleeve of his jacket and glanced down at his watch. It was 7:59 P.M, but a moment later the time changed to 8:00 P.M. His head darted up and down the alley looking for the crackhead that had sold him the bulletproof vest.

"Eight o'clock sharp my ass," Melvin said to no one in particular as he rocked back and forth on his shoes, taking a deep breath.

"Psssst!"

"What the fuck?" Melvin looked alive hearing the noise. Drawing a Swiss army knife from his jacket's pocket, he whipped around to where the sound had come from. His eyebrows were sloped and his nose was wrinkled. His fist was clenched at his side and he was ready to poke whoever up that posed a threat to him. He expected someone to be standing not too far behind him, but he didn't see a soul. That's when his eyes darted to their corners and he felt someone grab him by his shoulder. His eyelids stretched wide open and he whipped around, swinging his Swiss army knife.

"Argh, fuck!" Crackhead Jerome belted out and grabbed his hand in pain. Melvin had just sliced open his palm and it was oozing blood, drizzling on the ground. A couple of droplets hit the tip of his tattered Reboc sneaker. He balled his wounded hand into a fist and tucked it under his arm. "Goddamn it, sssss, fuck that shit hurt! What the hell is your problem?"

"You can't be creeping up on niggaz like that, homie. I thought you were somebody trying jack my ass out here. You know this hood's rep?"

"Of course I do." He said in pain.

Crackhead Jerome squeezed his eyelids shut and clenched his jaws to fight back the fire in his palm. Afterwards, he peeled his eyelids back open and reached into the small of his back. He pulled out something wrapped in a red washcloth ans passed it to Melvin. A frowned up Melvin looked down at the cloth wondering what it was concealing. Figuring that it had to be the gun that he requested, he closed his knife and slid it into his back pocket. He then took the cloth and slowly unfolded it. Once he was done unfolding it, he had an old Colt Peacemaker in his hand. Creasing his forehead, Melvin looked back and forth between the vintage pistol and the crack fiend. He wasn't really feeling the weapon. It looked like something out of the old western days.

"Fuck is you looking at me like that for? You said you wanted a piece with no bodies on it, right? Well, there you have it."

"Where you get this from?" Melvin inquired, turning the Colt over and examining it in the cloth that it was given to him in.

"What does it matter? Now, do you want the goddamn thing or not?" Crackhead Jerome asked. He was hostile now that he'd gotten his hand sliced. All he wanted was his money so he could get high. He knew that once he beamed up that he'd be okay. Tomorrow morning he'd take himself up to the emergency ward down at Martin Luther King hospital to get his hand sewn up.

"Does it work?" Melvin raised an eyebrow.

"Yeah, it works. Hell would I sell you a piece that doesn't work for?"

"Crackheads aren't exactly trustworthy people, you know?"

"Whatever, man. I'm not finna be standing here while you insult me and shit. Look, I even brought you some bullets for the mothafucka," he pulled out a small black bag of bullets from inside of the hoodie he was wearing and passed it to him. Melvin took a peek at the bullets inside of the black bag. He then loaded the chamber of the Colt with rounds to make sure they fit. Satisfied, he tied the black bag up and stashed it inside the pocket of his jean jacket. "Alright, how much do you want for her?"

"Gemme two large, man," Crackhead Jerome said to him, then looked up and down the alley to make sure that they weren't being watched by anyone.

"One fifty."

"Nah, two hunnit, take it or leave it."

"Leave it," he tried to hand him the pistol and bag of bullets back, but he wouldn't accept them.

"Alright, alright, alright," Crackhead Jerome fell back from his firm price, "Gemme the one fifty."

Melvin tucked the pistol under his arm and reached inside of his pocket. He pulled out a small wad of folded dead presidents and counted out the money he'd made the deal for. Once he had the bills counted up, he passed them off to the crack fiend and watched him look it over. Once the smoker fool had figured out that he had the right amount, he stuffed the bills inside of his pocket.

"Look, you know anyone that may wanna rocket launcher?" He asked in a hushed tone.

Melvin frowned up and said, "Now, who the fuck would I know that would wanna buy a goddamn rocket launcher? Hell no, I don't know nobody. Aye, man, nice doing business witchu, I gotta go." He thanked him and held up the pistol which was still enclosed inside of the cloth. He then tucked it at the front of his pants and went on about his business down the alley. Reaching his vehicle, he jumped in behind the wheel and cranked it up. A moment later, he was driving off.

As soon as he was out of sight, Jerome made his way out of the alley and headed down the block where the two niggaz in the doo-rag and fitted cap were earlier that day. He bought crack off the dude in the fitted cap that had threatened to pop his smoked out ass and went on his way.

Tranay Adams

## CHAPTER EIGHT

Melvin stood before the mirror of his nightstand. He had a black bandana over the lower half of his face and a Colt peacemaker tucked in the front of his slacks. He put on his most menacing scowl and drew his pistol repeatedly. He tucked, pulled, tucked and pulled it, trying to shorten his draw time, each time he pulled it out and pointed it.

"Bet notta mothafucka in here move!" Melvin drew down on the mirror once again and pointed his pistol at it. He then waved it around, like he was inside of a room with a few people. "Alright now, you right there in the beanie, I want chu with your hands high up in the air, reach the ceiling goddamn it, or so help me I'll fill yo' punk ass with some hot shit! As for the rest of you niggaz, I want chu on your stomachs with your hands on the back of your heads! Do that nice and slow, reallll nice and slow! That's right, just like that! Now, you in the beanie, take me where ever you keep the money and drugs, and if you try anything funny that's gone be yo' ass!" He narrowed his eyelids at the imaginary person and squared his jaws. Afterwards, his shoulders slumped and he released the tension from his body. The hostility drained from his face and he pulled the black bandana down around his neck. "I got it, I got it. I can do this. All I gotta do is make these mothafuckaz believe that I'll pop one of 'em, and the rest will be a breeze, like taking candy from a baby." He said as he paced back and forth across the bedroom, removing and placing the hammer back into place over and over again.

*Knock! Knock! Knock! Knock!*

Hearing knocks at the door, Melvin hurriedly took off the black bandana that was around his neck and wrapped his pistol up in it. He darted over to the mattress and lifted it, stashing the weapon underneath it. He then stripped down to his wife beater and boxers, tossing his clothes on the floor beside his bed. Grabbing his remote control from off the dresser, he turned the TV on to some old western flick. Next, he ran over to the mirror on the nightstand, where he wiped the sheen of sweat from his forehead with the back of his hand and looked himself over. After taking a deep breath, he shut his eyelids briefly and advanced to the door. He opened the door and found Tiaz on the other side.

"You straight, pop? I thought I heard shouting in here?" Tiaz frowned, looking around the cracked open door.

"That was the TV," Melvin lied, wagging the television's remote at him. Once his son took in the wife beater and boxers that his old man was wearing, he concluded that he was telling the truth.

"Oh, okay, well, me and Cameron about to go see these girls from around the way."

"Alright, son, be careful."

"I love you, pop."

"Alright," He shut the door behind his son and approached his bed, lying across it. He sat his remote control down on the dresser and interlocked his fingers behind his head, staring up at the ceiling. He couldn't help thinking about how his first stickup was going to play out. The thought alone made butterflies come to life in his stomach.

*\*\*\**

Haa! Haa! Haa! Haa!

Tiaz and Threat breathed heavily as they sprinted down the dark alley. Their faces were shiny and masked with perspiration. Their chests heaved up and down and their lungs felt hot. Their legs were aching having run so long but they dared not stop because if they did that would have been their asses.

Threat looked to Tiaz as he lagged beside him. He was tired as shit and looked like he was about to collapse. However, the echoes of a thunderous crowd caused his head to snap over his shoulder. Those angry niggaz were hollering and yelling insults as they drew closer.

"Come on, T, keep up." Threat yelled over his shoulder to Tiaz.

"Ahhh!" Tiaz fell to the ground, looking as if he was about to faint. He was so exhausted. "Haa! Haa! Haa! Haa!" He panted out of breath as he looked up at Threat trying to pull him up, all the while checking to see if their nemesis were still on them, they were.

"Get up, man! We've gotta get outta here!" Threat struggled to get him on his feet and moving again.

"Gone, Threat, I'm through! I can't hack it no more." Tiaz waved him along. "I'm done, go on without me."

"Nah, fuck that!" Threat pulled his comrade up to his feet and leaned him up against the brick wall inside of the alley. He looked ahead and their adversaries were still charging after them, their numbers swallowing up the dark path. They wanted blood, their blood.

Threat's head darted all around the alley trying to find something they could defend themselves with. He spotted an empty clear glass bottle of Captain Morgan on the ground beside a trash bin. Snatching it up, he shattered the end of it, creating a jagged edge and a lethal weapon. He tossed the broken bottle over to Tiaz, and he tested it out, jabbing it at an imaginary body and head. When Threat looked up he saw a 2 X 4 sticking out of the same trash bin. He pulled it out and practiced swinging it as if it were a baseball bat.

"Here they come!" Tiaz alerted Threat before springing into action.

*Sniktttt!*

"Gaaaahhh!"

71

One of them staggered back grabbing his face with both hands after meeting the jagged edge of Tiaz' broken glass bottle.

*Sniktttt!*

"Arghh!" Another one grabbed his cheek, the meat hung and blood slicked his fingers.

*Crack! Whackk! Bwhackkk!*

The 2 x 4 broke in half and sent splinters and debris everywhere. Threat had lifted the last of the men off of his feet. He came flying down on his back, legs going up in the air and eventually falling back down. They fought on courageously and were holding their own until a loud noise stopped them all.

*Bop! Bop!*

The report from the handgun froze everyone in their tracks. They looked up to find a skinny light skinned nigga with a Mariner's *S* tattooed between his eyes. He sported his long hair in pigtails and a barely visible goatee framed his mouth.

"You two niggaz don't move, cuz!" Pigtails moved his gun between Tiaz and Threat. His homeboys pulled their wounded to their feet and ushered them off to the sidelines. "Drop the bottle." He ordered Tiaz and he obeyed. He and Threat stood there with their chests swelling and deflating as they breathed hard from the rumble. "Now y'all gone stand there while my Locs beat ya'll asses or I'ma leave you in here stinking, feel me?" Although he didn't receive a response, he knew the young hoodlums understood him. He gave his Locs the nod and they swarmed their prey.

"Ooof!" Tiaz dropped to his hands and knees from a gut punch.

"Ahhh!" Threat was slammed against the trash bin from a forceful punch to the face. Then he was slung to the ground beside his partner in crime. All they could do was ball up into fetal positions as they were kicked, stomped, and punched. Once they were handed down their ass whoopings, Pigtails tucked his banga on his waistline and approached them, unzipping his Dickies.

He smiled fiendishly as his swept his limp dick between Tiaz and Threat pissing on their faces and bodies. After he was done, he stashed his meat and zipped up.

"Marks," He kicked Threat hard but Tiaz even harder. He threw up his set and motioned for his gang to follow him as he walked off down the alley, leaving both men unconscious.

An hour later Threat was groaning as he was rubbing the back of his head. His eyelids peeled apart and the sky was a murky blue with the sun beginning to rise. He looked to his hand and it was slicked red. He looked to Tiaz and found him wincing and moaning as well. He scrambled over to him.

"Yo, Tiaz, are you alright, man?" He hunched over him trying to shake him conscious.

Tiaz eyelids slowly peeled open and he looked up at Threat. He then looked all around trying to figure out where the hell he was.

"Nah, I'm fucked up. I think my fucking ribs are broken."

"Come on, we gotta get chu to a hospital." Threat pulled Tiaz up to his feet and threw his thick muscular arm over his shoulders. Holding him about the wrist and waist, he walked with him down the alley.

"You didn't leave me, Threat. You coulda bounced on a nigga but chu didn't. That's love."

"You're my brother; I'm always down for you. Like you're down for me, right?"

"Right. 'Til the death of us."

Tranay Adams

## CHAPTER NINE

After the beating Tiaz and Threat were given by the hands of the sixties, instead of going to the hospital or home, they decided to spend the remainder of the night getting high. After they'd finished, they dapped one another up and went their separate ways.

Tiaz came through the front door of his home looking like he'd been through hell and back. He shut the door behind him and touched his bottom lip, coming away with blood. Fuck, he cursed under his breath and removed his jacket. Having hung it up on the coat rack by the door, he made his way inside of the kitchen and opened the refrigerator. The first thing he grabbed was one of his father's ice cold Genuine Drafts and placed it on the growing lump on the side of his head. Shutting the door, he turned around to find the back door opening and his father stepping through it. He could tell that he'd just finished smoking because he was blowing smoke from out of his nose and mouth.

Melvin closed and locked the door behind him. When he turned around and saw his son, he was taken aback a little. A line creased his forehead as he approached him. He grabbed him by his chin and turned him from left to right, examining his injuries, carefully.

"Lemme guess, I don't wanna see the other guy, right? Oh shit, son, you smell like hot piss." Melvin took a step back, frowning up and pinching his nose shut.

"My bad, pop." He looked to the clock on the stove and saw that it was 9 o'clock in the morning. "OG, you been up all night?" His brows furrowed.

Melvin bowed his head and took a deep breath as he rubbed the back of his head. "Yeah, gotta lot on my mind, son."

"You wanna talk about it?"

"Nah, I'm good. Anyway, you wanna tell me what happened to you?" His father changed the subject.

Tiaz gave his father a quick rundown of what had happened that night. Afterwards, he had him take a shower. The young nigga found himself standing up inside of the tub with his head bowed. The hot liquid sprayed against his head and ran over his muscular form. The water rinsed off the soap that masked his body and sent it swirling down the drain.

"I bet that shower is doing your body some good, ain't it?" Melvin said, stepping back inside of the bathroom with a news paper tucked under his arm. He lifted the commode's lid and pulled down his pajama pants, plopping his bare ass on the seat.

"Yeah, it does help a lil'," Tiaz replied, sweeping the excess water from off his face. His nose twitched and he frowned up, smelling something foul in the air. "Damn, pop, that's you smelling like that?"

"Sorry, son, I had enchiladas today, you know how that goes." Melvin sprayed some Glade Lavender air freshener into the air. He then set it down on the bathroom sink and unfolded the news paper and looked it over.

"When you done, I'ma tend to your wounds. After that, I'm taking my tired black ass to bed."

"I hear that, OG. I'ma lay it down too. I done had one hell of a night."

"You sure have. And don't worry about them ol' punk ass niggaz that jumped you and Cameron either. Y'all gone catch up with one of 'em. Trust me. The universe always balances everything out. You just watch and see what I tell you."

"I hear you, pop. May the Lord have mercy on them fools souls when I catch 'em 'cause I'm sure as hell not." Tiaz winced having touched the lump at the back of his head.

"Oh, I believe you," Melvin said, flipping through the news paper. "My boy doesn't play that, and neither did his godfather. My street brother may have beena square, but there wasn't too many that could see 'em with the hands. It's funny 'cause you remind me of him in some ways. Y'all not only share some of the same personality traits, but the same name as well. Hell, he's probably living through you."

*Melvin gangsta leaned in his '76 Cutlass Supreme, nodding his head to George Clinton's 'Double Dutch Bus'. He had on an apple jack and a wife beater, which he wore suspenders over. Melvin was smiling from ear to ear. It was Friday; he had a pocket full of dead presidents and the baddest broad in the city. Niggaz couldn't tell him nothing. As far as he was concerned, he was most definitely the fliest nigga there ever was.*

*The sun was beaming brightly, shining light on his ride. Although the vehicle was old, the mothafucka looked brand spanking new. Its last owner, a white dude that thought he was cooler than the other side of the pillow, kept up with the maintainence of the automobile. It ran like a champ.*

*The only reason why the white dude had sold the car was because he was locked up and needed money for an attorney for a charge he was fighting.*

*Melvin took in all of his surroundings as he cruised through the streets, smiling and waving at niggaz that he knew from off the streets. Women were giving him the eye and trying to flag him down, but he already had a lady, so he didn't have any holler for them. A block and a half later, Melvin found himself sitting up and narrowing his eyelids. He thought that he saw someone that he knew coming up at a bus stop, on his right hand side.*

*"Hold up," Melvin turned down the radio and peered closer through the windshield. He turned the volume down like it was going to help him see better or some shit. "I*

know that ain't my nigga Tiaz." He smiled harder. "That is that nigga. Lemme swoop up on 'em, right quick."

Melvin hit his turned signl and made a right turn. He pulled up on Tiaz who was in the middle of talking to a little brown skinned honey. He could tell from the way she was smiling that she was feeling what Tiaz was saying. This didn't surprise Melvin though. His homeboy had always been a ladies man.

"What's happenin', homeboy?" Melvin smiled and threw his head back like What's up? When Tiaz turned around and saw his right-hand man, he smiled from ear to ear.

"What it is? It's beena minute, my nigga." Tiaz said, hunched down so he'd be at eye level with his homie.

"I know. Take a ride witcho nigga one time, let's catch up."

"Fa sho', family, gemme a second," Tiaz pulled his backpack from around his shoulders and unzipped it. He pulled out a spiral notebook and an ink pen. He opened the notebook and passed it to the girl he was spitting his G at. Right after, he handed her the ink pen and told her to scribble down her math. Once she was done, he placed the items back inside of his backpack. Next, he took the girl's hand. Looking her square in her eyes, he kissed her hand tenderly. This caused her to blush. He then promised to give her a call, so that they could set up a time and day for them to hang out. "Take it easy, beautiful." He rubbed her hand as he stared into her eyes, licking his lips and biting down on his bottom one. He caressed the side of her face and then jogged over to Melvin's ride. He opened the front passenger door and hopped it, slamming the door shut.

"What's up, loved one?" Melvin smiled jovially as he gave his homeboy a complicated handshake.

"*Ain't 'bout nothing. You know me, maintaining and hanging. Nigga, on his school boy shit, so you know how that go.*"

"*I'm proud of you, my nigga. You know what I'm saying? You coulda been out here like me and the rest of the knuckleheads breaking bad, but chu chose school. My main man 'bouta be a doctor and shit.*" *He dapped him up.*

"*Thanks, man. This school shit ain't easy, but I'm making it do what it do. You feel me?*" *Tiaz let the sunvisor down and revealed the rectangle shaped mirror. He took the black power fist comb out of his unkempt afro and forked it out; making sure that it was fluffly. Afterwards, he patted it down to make sure that it was perfectly round. Satisfied, he put the sunvisor back up and stuck the black power fist comb back into his afro.*

"*It's 'bout time you cut that shit, bruh.*" *Melvin said, looking back and forth between his homeboy and windshield.*

*Tiaz looked at Melvin like he was bat shit crazy.* "*Nigga, pleeeease, I'll never cut my hair. If a nigga cut my hair off, I'll lose all my power and shit. Just like that nigga Samson outta the Bible.*"

*Melvin busted up laughing as he held his fist to his mouth.*

"*Yo' ass is extra'd out, my nigga. What chu gone lose if yo' wig get split?*"

"*Shiiiiit, my ability to fuck all these hoes,*" *He laughed and did the complex handshake he'd done with his man earlier again.*

"*You something else, man. I ain't laughed this hard in a while. That reminds me,*" *Melvin scowled and punched Tiaz in the arm. He instantly grabbed the sore area of his arm and looked at him like he'd lost his mind.*

*Tiaz balled his face up and said,* "*Oww, nigga, what the fuck wrong witchu?*"

"I ain't heard from yo' skinny black ass in a while, fool. You 'pose to be my ace. How you just gone up and disappear on me for two weeks and shit. Punk ass nigga, you ain't even answer my calls."

Tiaz stared at Melvin for a while, never uttering a word. Suddenly, he busted up laughing and smacking the dashboard, rocking back and forth in the passenger seat. This caused Melvin to frown up at him.

"Fuck is so funny?"

"You, nigga, you sound like a scorned lover and shit. Why you ain't been answering my calls? I ain't seen you in a while." He laughed harder and held his stomach as he doubled over.

Melvin went from frowning to smiling and laughing. "Fuck you, fool. You know I don't roll with too many niggaz like that."

"Oh, yeah, what about that fool Ralph?"

"Man, that nigga always shacked up with Thelma. With his ol' pussy whipped ass, he don't ever wanna come outta the house. Nigga done turned into a hermit and shit."

Tiaz nodded and said, "But, nah, I been busy with school and dipping off with these broads when ever I getta chance. Mom's been telling me you been calling, and every time I say I'ma call yo' ass back, I wind up doing something else."

"You ain't gotta tell me, I know how it is."

"Glad you understand, man. I fucks witchu though. You still my nigga if you don't get no bigger." He dapped him up. "If you tryna kick it there's this party tonight off 111th and Normandie."

"111st and Normandie, huh? I can dig it. What time?" he fished out a half smoken joint from out of the ashtray and sparked it up. He then blew smoke out the side of his mouth.

*"Nine, but you know how we do. We gone fall through that bitch 'round eleven o'clock, if you rolling with me."*

*"Bet." He took another puff of the joint and passed it to Tiaz. He watched as his homeboy took it to the head a couple of times before blowing out a cloud of smoke, polluting the interior of the car.*

*"This that shit, right here," Tiaz passed the joint back.*

*"I know. I gotta couple ounces I'm moving. Be sure to tell whomever you know that's tryna buy."*

*"Off top."*

*Melvin indulged in the joint and made smoke waft around him.*

*"Watch oooout!" Tiaz shouted.*

*"Oh, shit!" Melvin's eyes bulge and he dropped his joint. Gripping the steering wheel with both hands, he slammed on the brake pedal and caused the vehicle to screech to a halt. He stopped right at the bumper of a Buick and sighed with relief. He lay his head back against the headrest and took a deep breath, heart racing.*

*"Shit that was close." Melvin said and looked at Tiaz. "You straight my nigga?"*

*"Yeah, I'm good." Tiaz nodded, heart beating fast.*

*The Buick pulled off and Melvin went right behind it. Seeing something on the floor on Melvin's side of the car, Tiaz looked over and saw a .44 Magnum revolver. The weapon gleamed under the faint rays of sunshine.*

*"That's you?" Tiaz nodded to the revolver he spotted on the floor.*

*"What?" Melvin frowned and looked down, seeing it. "Yeah, that's me. You wanna check her out?"*

*"Yeah."*

*"Go 'head."*

*Tiaz picked up the .44 Magnum and examined it. He kept it out of sight of anyone that may have been watching him as he opened its chamber. Inside he found hollow tip* copper bullets. With the flick of his wrist, he snapped the chamber of the pistol closed and aimed it down at the floor, closing one eye.

"This a bad ass piece, man." Tiaz complimented his friend.

"I know, homeboy, that's why I bought it." He capped with a smile.

Right then, a police siren went off and startled the two friends. Their eyelids stretched wide and their jaws dropped. Their hearts thudded inside of their chests and a million thoughts went through their mind.

The fearful expression on Melvin face quickly morphed to one of determination. His eyebrows sloped and his jaws squared. He gripped the steering wheel and looked over at Tiaz. From the look in his eyes Tiaz knew that his best friend was thinking about sending the police on a high speed chase. Had it been for him not having so much to lose, he would have given him the okay to do it. But since he had a future he'd be gambling with, he shook his head no and squashed any chances of escape.

Coming to an understanding, Melvin pulled over and waited for the police. One by one they ordered them out of the car with their hands where their eyes could see them. They then had them place their hands on the back of their heads and lay down flat on the ground. As the cold metal bracelets were snapped locked on Melvin's wrists, he saw his life flash right before his eyes. This was because he was a two time loser and looking at life imprisonment thanks to California's three strikes law.

\*\*\*

**Later that day**

Melvin sat in the small interrogation room with his wrist handcuffed to a metal table. He had been sitting there for hours, so his ass had fallen asleep on him. Occasionally, he'd adjust himself in his seat trying to get comfortable, but it would only help for a couple of minutes.

His buttocks falling asleep were the least of Melvin's concerns though. He had a life sentence looming over his head like a black cloud and it had him stressed out. In fact, if you saw him earlier, you would have sworn he'd aged ten years in the past four hours. But who could blame the poor bastard though? The way things were looking for him, it was possible he'd never see another sunrise again.

Melvin had everything from assault & battery to breaking & entering on his record. If he was hit with the weapon's charge it would be the final nail in his coffin. The only thing that could save his ass now was a miracle. And he was hoping for just that as he smoked on what was his fifth Newport.

Melvin had just taken another puff of his cigarette when the door of the interrogation room opened. Detective Hoit came waltzing in over the threshold with a fixed scowled on his red face. He was in a sand colored shirt and a striped tie that hung loosely around his neck. He wasn't even within five feet of Melvin, but he could smell the nicotine and coffee seeping from out of his pores. The stench on the stock built man made his stomach churn almost as much as his impending imprisonment.

Detective Hoit, the mean son of a bitch that he was, wanted to bury Melvin's ass under the prison. He had it in mind to just give him the gun charge since he was a felon and the car was in his name. The only thing stopping him was the fact that his African American partner, Detective Reignhart, was an ex street nigga himself.

See, Detective Reignhart left it up to Melvin and Tiaz who was going to take the charge for the gun. At this *moment, Melvin would find out whether his homeboy was going take the charge for him or let him ride it out.*

*Hoit came around the table and snatched the Newport from between Melvin's fingers and mashed it out in the ashtray. He then pulled up his pants and sat on the edge of the metal table, mad dogging Melvin.*

*"You have got to be the luckiest son of a bitch to have ever been pushed out of a cunt that I've ever seen. I mean, your black ass must have a genie or a lucky fucking rabbit's foot or something," Hoit waited for Melvin to respond, but he didn't. He just stared up at him with hatred dripping from his moist, red webbed eyes. Seeing that he wasn't going to say anything, he continued on. "Your friend in there, The L seven square that's going to school to be a fucking doctor," he pointed to the wall, which Tiaz was on the opposite side of in the other interrogation room. "Well, he's gonna take the bull by the horns for you. Now, I done all I could to try to convince him to tell us that the piece was yours, but the little fucker wouldn't budge, stupid fucking kid." Hoit looked away and shook his head. He couldn't believe that Tiaz was going to flush his future down the toilet for his friendship. "You know, Melvin, if you were any kind of friend, you wouldn't let your buddy there throw away his life over your charge. I mean, you're a street guy, am I right? You guys claim to believe in a code of honor, respect and loyalty. So, tell me, where is the honor in letting your friend do your bid for you, while you walk away a free fucking man?" He leaned over to Melvin, his hot breath blowing into his face.*

*There was a long silence between the two men until Melvin decided to speak again.*

*"If we're done here, I'd like to go, detective," Melvin held up his shackled wrist and caused the chain of it to jingle. Hoit looked at him like he wanted to punch him square in the face, but he managed to calm himself.*

*Reaching inside of his pocket, he pulled out the handcuff key and unlocked the metal bracelet. Melvin stood to his feet, rubbing his aching wrist, which had a bruise around it from the cuff being on too tight.*

*** 

### Six months later

*Tiaz made his way across the prison floor giving what's up's to the niggaz that he knew and ignoring the rest. He was on his way towards the phones. He'd gotten halfway there when he locked eyes with a hefty correctional officer by the name of Chief Jackson. The two of them had a beef so they were mad dogging one another. Using his meaty hand, Chief swiped his hand across his throat, letting Tiaz know he was a dead man.*

*"Suck my dick, you fat sloppy body ass mothafucka!" Tiaz grabbed his bulge and shook it at him.*

*Chief scowled and twisted his lips, saying, "Yeah, you gone get yours, watch and see, you lil' bitch. You just watch and see." He promised with a dead serious look dripping from his eyes.*

*Tiaz held up his middle finger and kept it moving. He found himself standing in line along with the other inmates waiting to use the telephone. His afro was now braided into six frizzy cornrows and he had swelling underneath his right eye, which he'd told the correctional officers he'd gotten from a slip and fall. Truthfully, he'd gotten the black eye from his many squabbles since he'd been on lock. Mothafuckaz tested his gangsta and found out that he wasn't anything to play with. See, Tiaz had always been nice with his hands. Hell, he had to. This was because at five foot six he was always the smallest of his company and niggaz was always trying to chump him.*

*Once it was Tiaz' turn at the telephone, he picked up the receiver and wiped it off on his jumpsuit. He then placed the call he had in mind and introduced himself once he heard a familiar voice pick up.*

*"What's up, homeboy?" Tiaz grinned.*

*Melvin stopped playing Nintendo and took the joint from out of his mouth. He then said excitedly, "Yooooo, what it is, loved one?"*

*"Ain't shit, my nigga, maintaining. Holding on like a hubcap in the fast lane."*

*"Glad to hear it, my boy. You got that change I dropped on yo' books?"*

*"Yeah, yeah, yeah, I got that. Good looking out."*

*"You ain't gotta thank me. For what chu doing for me, it's the least a nigga could do. You feel me?"*

*"No doubt. So, how's the fam?"*

*"Oh, they straight, Kim waddling around here like a duck and shit."*

*"Shut up!" Kim mushed him and kissed his lips. "Who is that?"*

*"Tiaz."*

*"Oh, tell 'em I said hey, and we gone do it big when he comes home. We gone throw him a nice lil' get together soon as he touches down." She said excitedly. She knew what he'd done for her family and she wanted to show him just how much they appreciated it.*

*Melvin told Tiaz exactly what his lady said and vise versa. "He said he's looking forward to it."*

*"Okay. Well, lemme gone in here and whip my baby up something to eat."*

*"I'm not hungry, babe."*

*"Not chu, silly, my baby," she corrected him and placed her hands on her round belly.*

*"Girl, gemme a kiss and get on outta here."*

*They kissed, and he smacked her on her ass as she proceeded toward the kitchen.*

*"It's nice to hear y'all getting along over there." Tiaz smirked.*

*"Yeah, man, we're both excited about the new addition. We gotta start thinking of baby names."*

*"You know what y'all gone have?"*

*"Not yet. I'll let chu know once we do. You most def' gone be the godfather though."*

*"That's what's up. It will be an honor."*

*"We gone do a ceremony and everything to make shit official."*

*"Cool."*

*Melvin and Tiaz chopped it up a little while longer. He told him everything that had been going on with everyone on the outside since he hadn't talked to him for a while. The conversation took a turn for the worse not long after though.*

*"I love you, Mel."*

*Melvin's forehead creased and he said, "I love you too, my nigga. But what's up? That's like the fifth time you told me you love since we been on the jack."*

*"Ain't nothing wrong, homie. What, a nigga can't tell his ace he got love for 'em? Damn."*

*"Nah, it ain't like that. You know you and me go back like foe flats. It's just that...never mind."*

*"Yo',man, if anything should happen to me in here, I want chu to make sure I'm dressed to the nines for my funeral. I wanna be buried in an all white suit, hat and cane. I want my body rode through the hood in a horse and carriage. I want my coffin to be made up to look like an old school Cadillac Deville, perferably the 1972 model. And I want like a hunnit doves released after my ceremony. Send a young nigga out in style. You feel me?"*

*"Whoa, whoa, whoa! You talking just a lil' too crazy for my taste. You're starting to scare me. Where has all of this shit come from about chu dying? I don't like that, Tiaz. Don't talk like that."*

*Tiaz chuckled and said, "Bruh, you taking shit just a lil' too seriously. I'm just saying this shit in case something happens to me. You never know what could happen, especially in this hell I'm in."*

*"I hope that's all it is. I really do."*

*"Just so you know, I don't regret doing what I did for you. I know that if the shoe was on the other foot, you woulda done the same."*

*"In a heart beat."*

*"I love you, my nigga. Don't ever forget that."*

*"I won't, and I love you, too."*

*Melvin disconnected the call and mashed out what was left of his joint inside of the ashtry on the coffee table. Lying back on the couch, he stared ahead as tears pooled in his eyes. He read through the lines. Today would be the last time he spoke to his best friend again.*

*"Baby, what's wrong?" A frowned up Kim asked from the kitchen doorway with her hand on her belly. When he didn't answer, she sat down on the couch and rested his head on her breasts. She then kissed the top of his head and caressed his back lovingly. He cried and cried, never uttering a word to her about the conversation between him and Tiaz.*

Melvin stared ahead at nothing. He looked like he was in a trance as he rubbed his hand up and down his tattooed arm. The ink he'd gotten was of a block styled cross with a crown sitting on it sideways. At the bottom of it was *Rest In Paradise Tiaz Montgomery.*

As he stared ahead, Melvin's eyes slowly manifested with tears. He looked to be on the verge of crying until he blinked his tears back. He bowed his head and Tiaz gripped his shoulder firmly, looking down at him.

"You okay, pop?" He asked his old man.

Melvin took a deep breath and looked up at his son. Although he looked sad, he still managed to muster up a smile.

"Yeah, I'm good, son." He said to Tiaz as he picked up the news paper he'd dropped during his recalling of his best friend's final days.

"Okay, well, I'ma let chu wrap up in here. I'ma go get dressed so you can tend to my injuries." Tiaz adjusted his towel on his waist and headed out of the bathroom. His upper body was covered with beads of water.

Melvin wiped himself and flushed the toilet. Turning on the faucet, he lathered up his hands with soap and began rinsing them off. As he did this, he looked up in the medicine cabinet's mirror at his reflection. His reminiscing made him remember why he never told his son he loved him. It seemed like everyone he told that died. His parents, who died in an automobile accident once he moved to Killa Cali, his wife, Kimberly, Tiaz and a host of friends. They all died, and he couldn't help believing that it was because he told them he loved them and cursed them.

Life could be ugly sometimes.

Tranay Adams

## CHAPTER TEN

Melvn didn't have any idea who the first nigga was he was going to rob, but he did know that he wasn't about to jack any civilians like himself. Hardworking, nine to five, clock punching men were going to be pardoned from his exploits. Yeah, they'd get a pass, but everybody in the street life was fair game as far as he was concerned. He was gone bring it to all of them niggaz that he ran across and show them no mercy.

One day while out on a run in his cab, Melvin past by the same corner he saw the dudes in the doo-rag and fitted cap at that were interested in buying the bulletproof vest from off Crackhead Jerome. Only this day, the dude in the fitted cap was out there serving crackheads while homeboy in the doo-rag watched his back. It appeared to Melvin that although their little operation was small it was ran smoothly. Their little corner was on fire. They were selling crack one-hundred miles an hour up the block. He estimated that they were clocking between four-hundred to six-hundred dollars a day. Now that wasn't much between the two of them once it was split down the middle, but if they were stacking their loot and they both kept it all in one place then Melvin would have a nice little bag on his hands once he put that gun to them. It was highly unlikely that they were saving their gwap though. Melvin reasoned it was because they were young niggaz. See, that day's youth, very much like the youth of today, didn't give a shit about stacking their chips. You know, putting their money away for a rainy day, so they'd have money for bail, attorney fees and ransoms in case a loved one was kidnapped? You know, all of the larcenous shit that comes with the game? Nah, these youngstas wanted to shine and stunt on their peers, so they were running to spend whatever cheddar they made as soon as they got it. Melvin would bet his last dollar that these two knuckleheads were blowing their paper on clothes, sneakers and jewelry. So his best bet was to run up on them, make them take them to whatever little money they had stashed and then have them tell him the whereabouts of their plug if they knew.

Parking his taxi cab across the street, and in the cut from the D-boys, Melvin studied them and their routine. He did this for three days straight, and found out the dudes names that were working the corner. The one rocking the fitted cap name was Shivs and the one in the doo-rag name was Pooh. Melvin also took note that they never changed or switched up their routine. They set up shop at 6 o'clock in the morning and they closed shop at 12 o'clock midnight. They also kept the money they made from hustling stashed not too far away. It was inside of a beat-up old white mop bucket stuffed with a dirty towel with a piece of tattered wood propped up against it. Once Shivs had finished with all of the crack rocks that he had on him then he would go to that bucket to get some more work. Through his investigation, Melvin also learned that Pooh was the lookout man and the gunner. Well, they both had gats, but Shivs' gun was there just in case they were overwhelmed.

Melvin wasn't much of a shooter, so he found himself at the gun range for two weeks straight. It was in that little time that he discovered that he was a pretty good shot. He had an almost marksman type aim, putting holes in whatever target he set his sights on. During this time, he went over his plan over and over again until it stuck inside of his head. Once he had everything down pact, he decided to make his move on a Thursday night.

Melvin switched license plates with a 1990 Chevrolet Caprice identical to his own. This was just in case someone made his plates and gave it to the police while he was on his caper. After making the switch, Melvin parked his vehicle on the side street where Shivs and his homeboy were hustling. Having thrown on his cap, black sunglasses and black bandana over the lower half of his face, he double checked the chamber of his Colt. Seeing that it was fully loaded, he closed it and looked at his hand. It slightly trembled with nervousness so he grasped it. Slowly, he removed his hand and the hand holding the revolver still slightly trembled.

"Fuck it," Melvin said under his breath in regards to his trembling hand. This was his first time jacking a mothafucka so he understood why he was uneasy. He just had to focus on the task at hand. *Get that money and get the fuck on,* is what he thought to himself before jumping out of the Caprice. Melvin slammed the driver's door shut and stepped upon the curb, looking all around him for any cops or possible witnesses. Seeing that there wasn't anyone in sight, he continued down the sidewalk, sneakers creeping up the black spotted concrete. As he neared the corner of the block someone smoking a cigarette and riding a bicycle came flying past him. The man on the bike turned his head in his direction, brows furrowing seeing how he was dressed. Melvin's heart was already beating fast, but after that encounter its pacing doubled. On top of that, the palms of his hands had grown damp. He started to hop back into his car and drive off, but he figured he was already en route, so he may as well go along with his plan.

Melvin crept around the corner just in time to see Shivs serving a crackhead. He glanced at the street just in time to see Pooh jogging across the street toward the liquor store he was at when he saw Crackhead Jerome trying to sell his bulletproof vest. This was good for him because it meant that he only had that nigga Shivs to worry about. As soon as Shivs had made the exchange he looked to his left to see Melvin. Although he couldn't see his face thanks to the light post's bulb being blown out, he figured he was there to buy the poison that he had for sell.

"'Sup, bruh? What chu need?" Shivs asked him. It was at that time that Melvin finally saw why he was called Shivs. It was because of the jagged scars going across his cheek and the one going diagonally across his neck. Melvin believed that he must have gotten them from prison. Although he didn't know whether he'd ever been locked up or not, it was just a guess.

"I need for you to gemme everything outta yo' pocket! And fork over whatever you got left in yo' stash!"Melvin drew his peacemaker and held it at his side. He spoke with dead seriousness, so homeboy knew that he wasn't fucking around. Still, it didn't stop homie from trying him. Shivs went for the Glock in his waistline. "Ah-ah-ah," he lifted his revolver so that it would be aimed at his forehead. Quickly, he glanced at the liquor store and saw Pooh paying for something at the counter, so he knew he had to hurry up. "Pull that shit out slow and drop it. And then kick it off the curb," he gave Shivs instructions and he followed them. When he thumbed through the wrinkled bills, he discovered that it was a few hundred dollars. "Good. Now, gemme yo' stash!"

Shivs mad dogged him, clenching his jaws so tight that they throbbed with anger. He looked like he wanted to strangle his ass, but he knew he didn't stand a chance with that pistol on him.

"Nigga, you gone have to kill me out here, 'cause I ain't giving you jack shit!" Shivs spat, nostrils flaring and chest jumping, with each breath that he took.

"Oh, I see you think it's a game, huh?" In a flash, Melvin cracked his victim across the bridge of his nose with the butt of his revolver. The impact broke the bone there and sent blood squirting out in spurts. Instantly, Shivs grabbed his fractured nose and slicked his hands wet with his own blood. His NY cap fell off his head and landed on the side of his sneaker. "You see? You see what that smart ass mouth got chu?" He kept his peacemaker on Shivs as he kicked the bucket over, spilling its contents. Once he saw the Ziploc bag of off white crack rocks, he snatched it up and stashed it in the front of his coat. "Alright, Mr. Shivs, you coming with me," he shoved his Colt into his back and led him to his vehicle, glancing over his shoulder to see Pooh receiving his change from his purchase. Once Melvin had his victim back at his Chevy, he forced him into the driver seat and ordered him to start up the car. Holding his revolver on him, he made him take him to his home.

"If you wanna live through this, youngin', you do exactly what I say when I say it. You don't gemme a hard time and you'll live to hustle again. Okay?"

Shivs was mad as hell. He didn't respond. He just sat behind the wheel frowned up and fuming. He looked crazy as hell with those scars on his face and his receding hairline. His nostrils were throbbing, and he was gritting his teeth, vein bulging at his temple.

"Nigga, do you hear me talking to yo' black ass? Don't make me nod you in this mothafucka, I'm not tryna have yo' death on my conscience." Melvin pressed his Colt against his temple, causing his head to tilt to the side.

"Okay, man! What the fuck, bro?" Shivs called out in a panic.

"That's more like it."

"Now, who you buy yo' shit from?"

"What?"

*Wap!*

He cracked him upside the head with the peacemaker causing him to grimace and hold the side of his head. He lost control of the car and had to swerve it back over into the lane.

"What the fuck, man? You gone make me crash this mothafucka and kill us both!"

"Take me to yo' plug's house, nigga!"Melvin roared, spittle flying from off his lips and sticking to the side of his face. Since Shivs was a nickel and dime hustling ass nigga, he knew that his supplier couldn't be that far up the food chain. He'd be someone that was fairly easy to get access to. And should this be true, he wanted all that mothafucka had...even the goddamn light bulbs out of the ceiling.

"Okay! Alright, damn!" Shivs steered with one hand and touched his temple a couple of times with the other, trying to see if he was bleeding or not. Once he found out that he wasn't, he shut his mouth and continued to drive. He went on to tell Melvin who his supplier was and one of the places he was laying his head. Satisfied with the information that he was given, Melvin settled down but kept his piece on Shivs.The rest of the ride was continued in an awkward silence.

Melvin found out that the nigga that was hitting Shivs off with his drugs was his sister's boyfriend. He'd set her up in a nice little spot on a hill over in Ladera Heights. From what Shivs told him he kept money and dope at the place. He'd slide through occasionally to check on things, but other than that he was rarely there, so his sister pretty much had the place to herself.

***

### 45 minutes later

Shivs stood outside the front door of his sister's home. He wore his fitted cap pulled low over his brows to hide as much of his injuries as he possibly could. His head was aching thanks to Mevin cracking him upside his head, and his nose had swollen something awful having been broken. Bluish black rings had formed under his eyes and over the bridge of his nose. He breathed funny and talked even funnier, but that was the least of his concerns. At the moment, he had Melvin standing at his back with his peacemaker shoved into his back. His hot breath was on his neck causing the hair there to stand.

"Alright, I want chu to knock on the door, should you try anything funny, I'll blow you and that bitch's brains out. Got it?" Melvin threatened. Shivs didn't say a word. He just arched his eyebrows and clenched his jaws. "I'm not in the habit of repeating myself, mothafucka. So I suggest you answer me," he gritted his teeth as he spoke into Shivs's ear, pressing his revolver further into his back.

"I got chu," Shivs rolled his eyes, annoyed. Taking a deep breath, he knocked on the door. When there wasn't any response, he waited for a moment, and knocked on it again. While he and Melvin waited for someone to answer the door, Melvin glanced over his shoulder to make sure there wasn't anyone watching them. There wasn't anyone in sight.

"Who is it?" Tamara, Shivs's sister's voice called from behind the door.

"It's me, sis…Wallace." Shivs gave her the name on his birth certificate.

"Who is that?" A very masculine voice came from the behind the door as well.

"Wallace?" The man sounded like he couldn't believe that her brother was there. "Fuck he won't? I told that nigga about just poppin' up! He know to hit my jack first!"

"I don't know," she said like she wasn't trying to argue with the nigga.

"Open the door for this nigga, man."

At that moment, Melvin readied himself because he heard the safety chain being taken off and the locks coming undone. As soon as the door came open, he saw a bald head dude in a sky blue and green bowling shirt and leather gloves. He lifted his Sig Sauer and popped twice, gun jerking in his hand and empty shell casings flying in the air. The first shot went wild and hit the door while the other struck Shivs in the stomach. He doubled over hollering in pain. Melvin kicked him in the ass and he fell forward, hitting the floor, carpet burning the side of his face. Seeing something silver gleaming at the corner of his eye, Melvin kicked the front door and it slammed into Tamara. She grimaced, feeling the impact of the door against her face. The force behind it broke her nose and sent a jolt of pain to her brain. She fell to the floor and dropped her nickel plated .32 while in freefall. As soon as her body met the carpet, a second wave of bullets was sent in Melvin's direction. He dove out of the way of the bullets and they went through the door, sending splinters flying every where.

Looking from where he was on the floor, Melvin saw homeboy in the bowling shirt about to take another shot at him. Reactively, his peacemaker came up spitting fire at him. The man threw his head back and hollered in pain as fire ripped through his shoulder, splattering blood against the wall behind him. Wounded, the man held his gun to his bleeding shoulder and ran inside of his bedroom.

Melvin got to his feet and kicked the front door shut. He then ran into the bathroom and slammed his elbow into the medicine cabinet's mirror, creating a cobweb and raining glass shards down into the sink. Using his gloved hand, he picked up one of the glass shards and ran back into the hallway. Placing his back up against the doorway, he eased the glass shard out into the doorway so that he could see inside of the living room. When he did this, he found homeboy rummaging inside of the closet for something. Peering closer, he saw the first end of an M-16 assault rifle he was taking down from the top shelf of the closet.

Recognizing that his life was in grave danger, Melvin dipped inside of the bedroom and put one in his calf. The bald head nigga hollered out, gritting his teeth and dropping the M-16. He went to pick up the assault rifle and he took one in his meaty buttocks. The wounded man hollered out in excruciation feeling the rip through his left ass cheek. Before he knew it he was getting grabbed by the back of his collar and a pistol was being pressed against his temple. He howled in pain feeling the hot barrel of the weapon against his flesh, sizzle his cheek like the ember end of a cigarette. "Where the money and drugs? I'ma only ask yo' bitch ass once." Melvin told him straight up, hoping he didn't try his hand because he didn't need a murder on his conscience.

"Alright, okay," bald head said, bleeding all over the carpet and shit. "It's…it's in the couch cushions, I'll needa knife to get to it."

"Okay, on your feet," Melvin pulled him upon his good leg and walked him like a limp dog inside of the living room. It was there that he found Shivs lying on his back and gasping for air, clinging for dear life. He didn't pay him any mind as he pulled his Swiss army knife from his back pocket and triggered the blade, passing it to his victim. The bald head nigga looked at the knife as he held it in his hand, seeing his reflection in it. It was from this that Melvin knew that he was thinking about trying his luck, so he thought it was best that he warned him. "It ain't even worth it, my nigga. Gone gemme what chu got and call it a night. You can live to hustle all of this lil' bit up again. You feel me? It ain't worth yo' life," With that said, the bald head nigga stabbed the knife into the fabric of the couch cushion, pulling it downward. His action caused the cotton stuffing to spill out of the opening he'd made. Using both hands, he ripped the cushion open further and discovered stacks of money inside.

Seeing the bowling ball bag on the side of the couch, Melvin emptied the dark burgundy bowling ball out of it and sat it down on the arm of the couch. Carefully, he watched as his victim stuffed the stacks of money inside of the worn brown leather bag. A smile stretched across Melvin's lips looking at all of the money that was being crammed inside of the bag. Through his peripherals, he saw homeboy cutting open the other cushion on the couch, revealing the top of something wrapped in cellophane. It was obvious a kilo of cocaine.

Melvin was so engrossed with all of the money inside of the bowling bag, that he hadn't noticed that the bald head nigga had pulled out a .9mm Taurus from the couch cushion he'd pulled all of the money out of. It wasn't until he saw something moving out of the corner of his eye that he turned and looked. He was just in time to see the scowling man going to point his gun. Before the bastard could get off a shot, Melvin was putting one through his forehead. The bullet exited out of the back of his skull, sending itty bitty pieces of brain and blood splattering on the stacks of money inside of the bowling bag.

"Nooooooo!" Tamara screamed bloody murder.

Melvin didn't pay her any mind whatsoever, he had zoned out, realizing he had murdered a man. He stood there looking between his Colt and the lifeless eyes of the bald head nigga. It was his first time catching a body. All he could hear was his heart pounded inside of his ears and the constant screams of Tamara. She was staggering to her feet holding onto something tightly.

"Jesus," Melvin said to no one in particular.

*I killed him! I fucking killed him! Calm down, Mel, get a grip. These mothafuckaz in here know the game they chose and what comes with this shit. Fuck 'em, let Jesus explain,* Melvin thought to himself, *yeah, that's right, let Jesus explain it.*

"Noooooo! Noooooo! Nooooo!" Tamara screamed and screamed with his hands up trembling.

Melvin wasn't thinking about that bitch though, his eyes were on the prize. He pulled out the kilo that was wrapped in cellophane from out of the ruined couch cushion and tucked it at the small of his back. He then zipped up the bowling bag and snatched it up by its handles. He went to move for the door and that's when thunder erupted.

*Pow! Pow!*

Melvin stumbled backwards from back to back gunfire, eventually falling on his back and lying straight out. Lying on the carpet, he saw Shivs lying near the door. He was still, and looking up at the ceiling, blood forming beneath him. *Dead!*

Melvin winced, feeling the soreness in his torso. He was thankful that he had worn a bulletproof vest. Otherwise, he would have been a goner.

A tear streaked face Tamara sniffled and lowered her smoking nickel plated .32, smoke wafting from its barrel. She let the small gun drop to the floor and ran over to her man. Getting down on her knees, she lifted him up by his neck causing blood to drip and brain fragments to fall out of the back of his blown out skull.

"Oh, baby, what has he done to you?" Tamara cried aloud, rocking the corpse of her fiancé back and forth. Her big teardrops fell and splashed on the horror written across his face. His eyelids were stretched wide open and so was his mouth.

*Bow!*

A spray of blood came from Tamara's head and she slumped over, looking like she'd fallen asleep while holding her deceased lover in her arms. Melvin pushed himself up from the floor and grabbed the bowling bag. He limped over to the front door while glancing down at the dead face of Shivs. Opening the door, he looked out to see a host of red and blue flashing lights heading in his direction, police car sirens blaring loudly. With the threat of getting caught looming in the air, he fled out into the night and left the bloody scene.

## CHAPTER ELEVEN

Melvin made his way inside of the house wincing in pain, Colt in one hand and the bowling ball bag in the other. Closing the front door as quietly as he could, he looked around the house from where he stood listening for his son. The house was silent so he figured that Tiaz was either asleep or out running the streets. With that in mind, he locked the door and placed the safety chain on it. Entering the kitchen, he sat the bag down on the kitchen table along with his revolver. He then removed his trench coat and sat it on the back of one of the chairs at the table. Next, he removed his shirt and took off the Kevlar bulletproof vest he wore underneath it. For the first time he noticed the two mashed up pieces of metal stuck to it, which were the bullets that Tamara had fired at him. He plucked the bullets from off the vest and smacked them down upon the kitchen table. Next, he placed the bulletproof vest down upon the kitchen counter and looked at the two bluish purple bruises on his torso he'd received as a result of the impact of the bullets. Touching the sore areas of his body caused him to wince. His forehead wrinkled and his nose scrunched up, as he squared his jaws.

"Sssss, shit! Bitch got me good," Melvin said of his encounter about forty-five minutes ago. Hearing footfalls attempting to quietly approach the kitchen, he looked up and saw a shadow nearing the doorway of the kitchen. Instantly, he went into defense mode, snatching a butcher's knife from out of the wooden knife block. A gleam swept up the length of the blade and it sparkled at its tip. His eyebrows sloped and wrinkles formed across the beginning of his nose. He clenched his jaws and the muscles throbbed in them.

*Mothafucka broke into my home, where my boy lays his head! You done fucked up, now yo' ass is leaving out of here in a body bag!* Melvin thought to himself as he slowly crept to the doorway of the kitchen where he saw the shadow slowly approaching. Melvin and the shadow were about to collide, when he swung out of the doorway and grabbed whomever it was trying to creep on him underneath his chin. Backing up against the wall, he placed his hand on the intruder's forehead and pulled it back. He then pressed the butcher's knife against his throat.

"You crept up in the wrong nigga'z house," Melvin growled and moved to slit the intruder's throat from ear to ear.

"Pop, wait, it's me…Tiaz," Tiaz said wide eyed and mouth wide open. He was clad in his boxers and a holding a Beretta in his hand.

Melvin's forehead crinkled and he said, "Drop ya gun, drop it!" He ordered Tiaz and he obliged. He then roughly spun the young man around so that he would be facing him. He took him in from head to toe. Realizing who he was, the hostility drained from off his face. He then took a deep breath and released the tension from his body. "Son, what the fuck is you doing creeping around here like that? I almost killed you."

"Pop, I didn't even hear you come in; I thought someone broke up in here. I was about to give you the business, for real for real." He bent down and picked up the Beretta, which was lying at his socked feet. When he came back up, he frowned seeing the bruises on his father's torso and the blood on his shoe that even his old man hadn't noticed. He then looked to the bag and gun on the table. It was then that he acknowledged that his pop's was tangled up in some street shit. Turning back around to his father, he examined his form looking for more wounds. "Pop, what happened to you?"

Melvin took a deep breath and headed back inside of the kitchen, saying, "It's a long story, son." He walked back over to the kitchen table, sitting the butcher's knife down and peeling off his gloves. When he looked up, his son was sitting his Beretta down on the seat of one of the chairs and grabbing the leather bowling bag. Melvin started to stop him, but he said fuck it. His son was a street kid and he knew there wasn't any lie that he could spin to try to make him believe other than what he was already thinking at that moment. He decided then to allow things to play out how ever they pleased.

Tiaz unzipped the bowling bag and revealed stacks on top of stacks of wrinkled money inside. The money had a beige rubber band on each respective stack to hold it in place. Some of the stacks of money even had speckles of blood on it. This was literally blood money.Tiaz pulled out one of the stacks and looked at it, turning it from front to back. He then dropped the stack of money back inside of the bowling bag and sat down in the chair, pulling it up to the table.

"Pop, uh," Tiaz began scratching the side of his head. "You mind telling me the deal here?"

"I'm sure you can put two and two together, son. The evidence is laid out right there in front you. I'm not even gonna attempt to insult your intelligence with a lie. You know better than that, I didn't raise no dummy," Melvin told his son, as he rummaged through the cupboards. He came down with a glass and a bottle of Jack Daniels. He sat the items down on the table and grabbed a handful of ice from out of the freezer, which he dropped inside of the glass. Sitting down, he poured himself up a glass of the strong, dark alcohol.

"Alright," Tiaz folded his arms across his chest and nodded, as he looked over everything at the table. Coming up with an idea of what his father was doing now to make his money, he looked back up to him. "You running up on niggaz making them lay it down for yours. In other words, you out here jacking niggaz for a come up?"

"Well, that's one way to look at it," he responded, pouring up a second glass of alcohol. Once he was done, he took the liberty to slide the glass before his only son.

"Well, what's another way?" The young man picked up the glass that was poured for him.

"That I'm a hood I.R.S agent, I'm auditing drug dealers out here 'cause they ain't paying their taxes."

Tiaz smiled and took a sip of the dark liquor. It caused his face to wrinkle as he frowned up, turning his bottom lip upside down. The liquid fire poured down his throat and spread flames throughout his stomach. He sat the glass down on the table and wiped the liquor dripping from his lip with the back of his fist. Seeing his son frown up like that made Melvin grin and dimple his right cheek.

"Aaahhh," Tiaz patted his hand against his chest. "Pop, I don't know how you drink that stuff. Goddamn!"

"You just got them virgin taste buds is all. I got chu by a few years, catch up. Then you and I can have a drink together." He took another sip of the liquor.

"Mannn, I'm cool. I'm not fucking with that shit no more. I'm good, O.G." The young man pushed his glass of liquor back before his father.

"I'm starting to catch a buzz and these wounds are beginning to feel numb. I guess this Jack is starting to kick in." Melvin took another sip of alcohol and sat the glass down. He then turned around to face his son, nestling his hands in his lap. "So," he took a deep breath. "Do you have any questions?"

"Yeah, why did you take it to the streets? Why this?" He asked curiously.

Melvin glanced up at the ceiling, taking another breath and looking back to his son. "I lost my job down at the Staple Center...working as a cabbie wasn't gone be enough to take care of home. So I had to do what I had to do to make ends meet, and here we are." He picked his glass back up to continue to indulge in his alcohol beverage. "Anymore questions?"

"Yeah, can I get down with you?" Tiaz asked, smiling from ear to ear.

For a time his father just sat there staring at the young nigga as he looked at him with hopeful eyes.

"As much as I'd like to have someone watching my back while I'm out there, I gotta say no, son. It's too risky, unh unh." He shook his head.

"Aww, come on, pop, lemme roll witchu. Two heads are always better than one," he rose from his chair and approached his father to plead his case. "Trust me; had I been there tonight to watch your back, you would have never gotten shot."

"Nah, junior, I already lost your mother. I can't even begin to fathom how I would feel if I lost you out there in them streets, especially if I was the one that brought you in. I don't need that kind of shit on my conscience. No, sir," he shook his head no. "I'll just have to manage on my own."

"Pop, you said it yourself; you need someone out there to watch your back. Why not have me, someone you trust? Someone that you know that's not gone turn around and pop you in yo' back once y'all done securing that bag at the end of the night. Let's keep it in the family. I mean, I see what chu saying about me putting my life in danger by getting down with yo' cause, but look at it this way, OG. I'm gangbanging, I put my life on the line day in and day out. My life is always in jeopardy and at risk in my occupation. So ask yourself, what's the big difference if you decide to let me get down with yo' operation? Hell, I'ma do what I want to do anyway, just like I was when you were working that square gig. You stay on the move, so you can't be around all the time to watch me. You feel me?" Tiaz stared into his father's eyes with his fingers interlocked with one another, pleadingly.

Melvin just sat there staring into his son's eyes, thinking things over. He had some valid points, so it was hard for him to debate them. He could stand firmly on what he said, but when he thought about it again. At least if he took him along on the capers he'd be able to watch him closely whereas if he was in the streets he'd be on his own. Thinking about it that way, he thought that maybe it wouldn't be so bad to let his son roll out with him on heists.

"Alright," Melvin nodded.

"Alright? I can roll?" Tiaz asked like he couldn't believe what he'd heard.

"Yes," he went to take another sip of Jack. That's when an excited Tiaz embraced him abruptly, causing him to spill some of the hard liquor. "Damn, junior, you made me spill some of this shit on my jeans. Fuck," he hurriedly rose from where he was sitting, looking down at the wet spot on his crotch.

"My bad, pop, I'm just excited. Thank you, thank you, thank you," he hugged him again, and lifted him up, causing him to wince from his wounds. Sitting him down, he kissed him on the cheek, and the older man smirked, happy that he could put a smile on his son's face.

"It's just me and you, pop. Me and you," Tiaz moved his finger between himself and his father, "I love you, man."

"Alright, son," he smiled and shook his head before taking a sip of Jack.

"Man, pop, you gotta nice lil' bag here," Tiaz said, as he looked through the bowling ball bag of dead white men again.

"That ain't all I got," Melvin told Tiaz and reached inside of the pocket of his trench coat. He pulled out Shivs' gold chains, watch and ring and handed them to his son.

"Hold on, pop, I'ma be right back." Tiaz left and came back with a loupe, which was something that jewelers used to check the clarity of diamonds. The young nigga held the loupe to his eye and went over every stone in the jewelry. "Pop, some of these stones in here are cloudy, but I know someone that will take the dope and jewelry off you."

"Cool. You hook me up with a fence and I'll cut chu in on a piece of the action."

"You gotta deal, OG." Tiaz smiled and dapped up his father. Tiaz took another look at the Colt peacemaker that his old man had used in the robbery/homicide, the bruising on his torso as well as the blood that was on the stacks of money inside of the bowling ball bag. His forehead creased with lines, as he couldn't help but wonder. "Pop, did you have to kill some people tonight?" He asked as if all of the pieces of the puzzle had fallen into place. It hadn't even dawned on him that his old man may have popped somebody over that bag he brought home when he asked about it earlier.

Melvin locked eyes with his son for what seemed like an eternity. It was through his eyes that he communicated to his offspring that he had indeed murdered some people. Breaking his son's gaze, Melvin took another sip of the Jack and sat the glass down on the table top.

"Come on," Melvin stated, pulling the bowling bag closer. "Help me count up this bag so I can see how much we working with here."

"We?" Tiaz raised an eyebrow.

"Yes, we, as in you and me, son, We a team now, so whatever we get we break bread with one another."

Tiaz pulled out a chair and sat down excitedly, rubbing his hands together greedily. He loved shooting the shit with his old man.

"Damn, pop, we gotta get us a money-counter, it's gone be a minute for we count up all of this shit."

"Got cha," Melvin pointed at his son. "Next time we'll make sure we have one of those, 'cause God knows I don't feel like running up all of this money."

Melvin chopped it up with his son for a while before heading off to his bedroom with a glass of Jack in his hand. He stripped down to his boxers and picked up a tube of A & D ointment, sitting his glass down on the dresser. Sitting down on the bed, he removed the cap from the tube and oozed some of it out onto his finger. He then rubbed the ointment in on the bruises that he got as a result of being shot back at the home invasion. At this time, he couldn't feel the tenderness of his bruises because the liquor had him feeling real nice. Seeing the portrait of him and his wife on their wedding day sitting on the dresser, he picked it up and stared down at it.

"I know you may not agree with me bringing our son into this game, but the way I see it I'd rather have 'em with me so we can watch one another's back. At least this way I can keep a close eye on 'em and know exactly what he's doing. Well, most of the time at least. I promise you that won't nothing happen to him that won't happen to me first. I'ma protect our boy at all costs, baby," he took a deep breath as his eyes pooled with tears, obscuring his vision. "God, I miss you, woman. I miss you, I miss you, I miss you so, so much. There's notta 'notha woman out there for me. I vow to give you the rest of my life. Another woman will never ever warm the other side of our bed. I swear before God Almighty when I lost you, I lost a part of me that I will never get back again. And the only reason that I haven't came to join you is 'cause our son was born. But fret not, my love, 'fore we will be reunited again, and I swear on a stack of Holy Bibles to love you even more than I have ever loved you on this earth...if that's even possible." Tears slicked down his cheeks and dripped onto the portrait, splashing on the glass of the picture frame.

When he turned off the lamp light, the illumination of the light post out on the street shined in through the window. This gave him a blue hue. Turning on his side, he held the wedding portrait against his chest and curled into a fetal position. Melvin tucked his chin to his chest and shut his eyelids. His lips quivered and tears cascaded down his face. He whimpered in great emotional pain.

"My baby, my sweet, sweet, sweet, darling Kimberly," he continued to cry as his entire body shuddered.

Melvin cried more than the day he cried when his wife died until he'd fell asleep, dry white tears on his face.

## CHAPTER TWELVE
### *The next day*

Melvin and Tiaz had just left a cat that they sold off the jewelry and the block of yayo to. They busted the bag down the middle, splitting it 50/50. Although Tiaz wouldn't accept the money at first, his father insisted and he finally submitted. *If one eats then we all eat,* Melvin told him.

"I gotta get rid of this pistol; it's hot as a fire cracker," Melvin said from behind the wheel of his taxi. "The last thing I want to do is get caught with this bad boy."

"Yeah, pop, I know you not tryna end up in county fighting homicides, you liable to be down for years even if they don't stick you with a case." Tiaz informed him. "Shiiiit, man, I got homies that's been on lock for three, four years fighting bodies that's not even their's. Shit crazy."

"Well, when I get rid of this piece I most definitely gone needa 'notha one. You will too for that matter."

"You in good hands, OG," Tiaz smiled and patted his old man on the shoulder. "I know somebody we can see, if it's burners you need. My man Gatz got plenty of toys and at an affordable price, too."

"Affordable, huh?" Melvin capped with a smile. "I like the sound of that. We gotta get rid of this piece first, though."

"Pop, we can just toss that bitch into the gutter." Tiaz stared out of the passenger side window, watching the streets pass him by in flashes.

"Good idea," Melvin grinned, snapping his fingers and pointing to his son.

Melvin pulled up alongside a storm drain and handed Tiaz the murder weapon, which was wrapped up in a bandana. Tiaz opened the passenger door and looked both ways to make sure that there wasn't anybody watching him.

Once he saw that the coast was clear, he dumped the banga inside of the gutter. Afterwards, he shut his door and his father pulled off.

"Now, about this friend when all the guns you were telling me about," Melvin brought the conversation back up.

"Oh, yeah, Gatz," Tiaz remembered their discussion. "He doesn't live to far from here. Make a right at this corner right here, pop."

Before Melvin knew it he was pulling up outside of a big ass house. Standing out front, on the bottom step, was a short big head nigga. He had a brown hue and six neat cornrows that were pulled back and tied off by black rubber bands. The braids were pulled so tight that they made his forehead appear larger. The twenty year old had acne scars on both cheeks and long chin hairs. He was dressed down in a white T-shirt which he wore underneath a green army jacket and leather combat boots. The thin gold necklace that hung from his chest was an AK-47 with a banana clip. The piece slightly gleamed beneath the sunlight provided from above.

"'Sup, my boy?" Gatz smiled. He slapped hands with Tiaz and gave him a gangsta hug.

"Ain't shit, you know how I do. Getting it how I live."

"Right, right, right," Gatz nodded as he understood where his homeboy was coming from. He was on the same shit that he was on. "'Sup, Mr. Petty? How are you?" The young gun merchant shook Melvin's hand firmly.

"I'm doing alright, Timothy, how about you?" Melvin released his hand and brought it back down beside him.

"I'm maintaining, sir. I can't complain."

"Glad to hear it," he checked his surroundings, giving his son some time to spring on Gatz exactly what they were there for.

There was an awkward silence as Gatz looked from Melvin to Tiaz scratching his chin. He wanted to ask them what they wanted, but he didn't want to come off as rude. He had the utmost love and respect for Tiaz, and being that they were homeboys that same love and respect extended to Melvin as well.

Tiaz looked back at his father to see what he was doing. He then turned back around to Gatz, nudging him and asking him to step somewhere out of the earshot of his father so that they could talk. The young man agreed and they stepped over near the bushes.

"'Sup?" Gatz threw his head back slightly.

"Well, me and pop needa see yo' inventory, we tryna buy a couple of them thangs." He answered in a hushed tone.

"You and pop?" His brows furrowed. He looked from Tiaz to his old man. "Are you serious?"

"Nah, nigga, for play, play, you gone look out or what?" Tiaz reached inside of his pocket and pulled out a wad of bills secured by a rubber band. As soon as Gatz saw the money before his eyes, a smile stretched across his lips. He then rubbed his hands together greedily. If there was anything on earth that he loved more than money, he hadn't come into contact with it yet.

"Oh, yes, follow me," Gatz motioned for Tiaz to follow him before walking towards the back of his house.

"Come on, pop." Tiaz threw his head towards the back of the house, signaling for his father to follow him and his comrade.

Melvin made his way towards the backyard on the heels of his son. When they reached the backyard, Gatz opened the garage door and walked inside. He flipped on a switch and light shined on everything present. There was an array of things scattered throughout the storage space. It was a lot of junk stored inside, but this wasn't without purpose. Nah, you see, Gatz used the stuff to make shit look good. The garage was made up to hide the fact that he was running a very illegal business from his home. If the police came knocking, it wouldn't look like he was selling guns out from out of the place.

"Close that door behind you for me, Mr. Petty." Gatz turned around to a raggedy ass refrigerator. Once Melvin obliged him, Gatz motioned the father and son over as he walked to the refrigerator. Grasping the door handle of the refrigerator, he looked back at his homeboy and his old man. "Alright, ya'll, shop's open," he pulled the refrigerator door open and removed the door's panel. Inside there were handguns ranging from different shapes, sizes, and calibers, residing on hooks, "This just a lil' something, something. You feel me?" He smiled delightfully. The young nigga was very proud of his inventory. He absolutely loved his job. The little nigga actually got a rush selling guns and other weapons of destruction.

Gatz took the toothpick out of his mouth and leaned down, pulling open the drawers of the refrigerator. There were bullets, shotgun shells, and magazines stored inside. When he came back up, he opened the freezer door and exposed a variety of shotguns and assault rifles. Licking his lips, he stuck the toothpick back in his mouth and stepped aside, allowing his newest customers over take a look at all of his merchandise.

Melvin and Tiaz picked up different guns, examining them and checking to see how many rounds they held. They ended up settling on .9mm Beretta handguns, a couple of other weapons and some silencers. They also copped some extra magazines and boxes of bullets.

"Timothy, you wouldn't happen to have any bulletproof vests, would you?" Melvin inquired.

"Hmmm," the gun merchant looked out the corner of his eyes and massaged his chin, thinking on it. "You know what; I thought I maybe had one left. But I'm sure I sold it a couple of weeks ago, sorry, Mr. Petty."

"Fuck," Melvin looked off to the side, hearing the disappointing news. He then looked back up at Gatz. "Don't be sorry, son. Don't ever apologize about getting money, no matter how you getting it, 'cause these mothafuckaz out here ain't gone give you shit. You understand me?" He gave him a stern look as he wagged his finger at him, like a disciplining father would.

"Yes, sir," he nodded.

"Good man." Tiaz' father patted the young man on the arm. This was his way of letting him know that they were good.

"I like yo' pop's, man. He's cool people," Gatz told Tiaz.

"He's alright." Tiaz grinned. He was just fucking around though. "Nah, my old man is the greatest, I'm lucky to have 'em as my father."

Tiaz looked to his father and he grinned, tapping his fist against the left side of his chest. This is where his heart resided.

"That's love." Melvin stated before paying Gatz for their merchandise. He and his son dapped the gun merchant up and turned to leave. They had just approached the garage door when Gatz called them back.

"'Sup?" Tiaz threw his head back.

"Gemme a sec', I got something I want chu to check out. I just got these bitches in," Gatz ducked off somewhere at the back of the garage amongst the other junk. Although Melvin and Tiaz couldn't see him, they could see the boxes that he was lost amongst slightly moving. It wasn't long before Gatz was rolling out an army green footlocker on a dolly. A smile was plastered across the young nigga'z face like he knew something that his homeboy and his father didn't.

Gatz stopped the dolly before Melvin and Tiaz, sitting it up. He then popped its locks and raised its lid, revealing a cache of round grenades inside.

"Take a look at those babies, now how many niggaz you know got some of these on deck? You fucking with me or what, my boy?" Gatz looked from Melvin to Tiaz.

Melvin and Tiaz exchanged glances and smirked.

\*\*\*

Melvin and Tiaz stashed the weapons under the spare tire inside of the trunk of the car. They then hopped in and peeled off. Melvin drove along the residential block with the wind blowing inside of the vehicle, ruffling him and his son's clothing. The radio was on 92.3 The Beat, but they weren't listening to the commercial that was playing at the time.

"Well, pop, what do we do now?" Tiaz asked.

"We gotta get chu a vest, son. We can't be out here half cocked and shit. Fuck around and catch a chest fulla lead and that will be all she wrote. You picking up what I'm sitting down?"He looked back and forth between the windshield and Tiaz.

"Yeah, I got chu, pop, but where are we gonna getta vest from?"

"I don't know. I honestly don't know." Melvin shook his head. He then sat quietly as he drove through the streets, thinking. Abruptly, he recalled something. "Well, I'll be damned. Melvin, you stupid son of a bitch, how'd you forget?" He smacked himself upside the forehead and grinned. Tiaz' forehead indented hearing and seeing his father.

"What's up, pop?" He questioned with concern.

"This nigga I met, I bought my vest from him. He told me should I ever need anything else from him where I could reach 'em. Hold on," Still gripping the steering wheel, Melvin lifted his ass from off the driver seat and pulled out his wallet, handing it to his son. "Look where I keep the money at and see if you see a piece of paper with a number on it. Tiaz obliged his old man and held the piece of paper between his fingers, observing it.

"Jerome?" Tiaz looked to his father to see if he'd gotten the right piece of paper that he'd requested.

"Yeah, that's him." Melvin responded and pulled over alongside the curb after he crossed the intersection. He then took the piece of paper from his son. "I'll be right back. I'm finna call 'em and see if he can get his hands on a couple."

Melvin hopped out of his car and made his way upon the sidewalk, en route to the telephone booth. The booth was banged up and had torn stickers on the sides of it, from companies that were advertising their businesses on it. When Melvin stepped to the booth, he snatched up the reciver and wiped it off on his shirt. He then dropped a quarter inside of the slot. Looking back and forth from the piece of paper with Jerome's number on it, he punched in the digits scrolled across it. Afterwards, he turned around and looked at his car, watching his son bobbing his head to the music playing on the radio.

A smirk etched across Melvin's lips as he observed his boy and listened to the telephone ring.

*Melvin lay in bed beside Kimberly listening to his walkman and rubbing coco butter on her stomach. While he applied lotion to her protruding belly, she happily painted her finger nails with purple polish. As soon as she was done with the nails of her hand, she held her hand before her eyes and blew on them. She did this so they would hurriedly dry.*

*"So, what chu hoping for, babe? A boy or a girl?" Kimberly asked, painting the nails of her other hands now. When she didn't get a response from him, she looked up to*

*find him lip singing the words to the song he was listening to as he rubbed lotion on to her pregnant belly. Chuckling, she plucked the headphones from off his head and repeated herself. "I said, 'what chu hoping for? A girl or a boy?'"*

*"Now, you know I got my fingers crossed for a baby boy. The king gone need a prince to be the heir of his throne," Melvin smiled and took the headphones from her, planting them back on his head. He left one of the earpieces off so that he could engage in conversation with his lady.*

*"Yeah, yeah, yeah," she sang, still painting her nails. "All men want boys so they can be just like them. I know the deal."*

*"How 'bout chu? What chu won't? A baby girl?" He oozed more lotion out into his palm and applied it to her protruding stomach.*

*"Yep. But I'd want her to be a daddy's girl, like I was. God knows I loved the hell outta my daddy. He couldn't do any wrong in my eyes as far as I was concerned." She smiled, showing off her beautiful set of pearly white teeth and the small gap that she had between them.*

*"Yeah, I like that idea," Melvin claimed, finishing up the rub down that he was giving to her belly. He then took the nail polish from her and began on her toenails, painting them one by one. "You make having a lil' momma not seem so bad. I could see her now, my baby looking just like my baby," he smiled at Kimberly and she blushed, turning her head. She didn't want him to see how much he had her wrapped around his finger. "Look at chu blushing, look at my baby." He sat the headphones aside and switched hands with the bottle of nail polish. He crawled over to her and kissed her all of her face. This caused her to laugh and giggle. "Look at chu, babe."*

*"What?" She looked up into eyes smiling and showing off her dimples.*

*"All the love in your eyes; I can't believe after all these years you still look at me like the girl in high school with the crush on the captain of the football team. That's amazing. Truly, truly, amazing, and I hope that never changes."*

*"It won't,"* she cupped his face with her hands as she stared up into his eyes. *"And I can guarantee that 'cause I have never loved someone like I love you. When I think about it, it don't make no sense how much I love you. I think about you all day every day. When you go out to get a pack of smokes or to go for a walk, although, you only be gone for like an hour, I be missing you. I be missing you like you flew outta town to another state or something, or like you locked up and you not coming home for a minute. For real for real, I got it bad for you, babe. I don't got no holla for another nigga, I got the man I want to be with...for life."* When she said that, she kissed him romantically and the diamond in her gold wedding band gleamed. She then pulled her lips back from him and said, *"I love you."*

*"I love you, too."*

*"You sure?"*

*"I have never been so sure of anything in my life."*

*"Awww,"* she showed him that smile that always seemed to make his heart skip a beat. They then hugged and kissed again. Afterwards, he went back to painting her toenails. *"I tell you what, if it's a boy you'll name 'em, but if it's a girl I will name 'em. Is that okay by you?"*

*"Fa sho',"* he said, without looking up as he painted her toenails. *"You got any girl names in mind?"*

*"Hmmmm,"* she smiled as she bit down on her bottom lip and looked up to the ceiling, thinking of names, *"How about Brishae?"*

*"Brishae? I like that."* He smiled and nodded his approval.

*"And for the boy?"*

*At that moment, Melvin stopped painting her toenails and looked up at her. A serious expression crossed his face and he said, "If it's a boy then I'm gonna name 'em after my brother from another and best friend...Tiaz."*

Melvin was still smirking and looking at his son when Crackhead Jerome finally answered the telephone.

"Chelllllo, Casanova of the Ghetto speaking," the crackfiend came on the phone jovially.

## CHAPTER THIRTEEN

Crackhead Jerome stood out on the corner with a piece of cardboard hanging around his neck by a length of twine. The cardboard sign read *Help! Homeless and Hungry.* In his hand he held a Styrofoam cup that was partially filled with coins and a couple of one dollar bills. He wore shades that blind people wore and held on to a walking cane. Occasionally, a vehicle would pull up to the stop light and the driver would stick out their hand offering change or a one dollar bill.

An old silver, curly haired white lady had just dropped a five dollar bill into Crackhead Jerome's cup when he heard the telephone at the raggedy phone booth ringing aloud. As soon as Jerome heard the telephone ringing, he lifted his shades upon his head and darted over to the phone booth. As soon as he reached the booth, he snatched the telephone from its lever and rubbed it off on his shirt. Afterwards, he cleared his throat and placed the telephone to his ear.

"Chelllllo, Casanova of the Ghetto speaking," Jerome answered the phone jovially, sounding like J.J Evan from the *Good Times* television show. He then smiled and showcased his decaying teeth. "Heyyyyy, what's up, main man? What chu need?" He dumped the contents of the cup into his palm and shoved it into his pocket. Next, he sat the cup down on top of the telephone booth and propped his cane up against it, "Oh yeah? How many you need? I'll tell you what; I'll see what I can do. I ain't making no promises. Now, should I be able to fill this order where should I take it?" Jerome switched hands with the telephone and propped his elbow against the phone booth. He looked at the dirt that was caked up underneath his fingernails and flicked it out with his thumb. "Alright now, I got it. Bye." He disconnected the call and pulled out an ink pen and small black book from his back pocket. Having pulled off the cap to the ink pen, he placed the book against the telephone booth and wrote something on the page.

\*\*\*

### *That night*

"Damn, man, you was only able to get one?" Melvin said to Crackhead Jerome as they stood inside of his living room. While he was talking to the smoked out thief, Tiaz was standing off to the side trying the Kevlar bulletproof vest on.

"Yeahhh, man, them bitches just don't fall outta the sky. I went through hell trying to get my hands on that one, so consider yo' self blessed that I was able to make it happen." Crackhead Jerome told him.

Melvin took a breath and ran his hand down his face. "Alright, how much do I owe you?"

Gemme what chu gave me for the first one, chief."

Melvin pulled a folded wad of money out of his pocket and peeled off the same amount of money that he'd paid Jerome for the first bulletproof vest he'd bought off of him.

Jerome took the money and shoved it into his pocket, smiling. He didn't even bother to count it because he didn't believe that Melvin would try to beat him out of some money.

"Look here, if you need anything else, you got my number."

"Indeed, I do." Melvin slapped hands with Jerome and patted him on his back. "Thanks, bruh."

"Don't mention it."

Crackhead Jerome made his way to the front door, hearing Tiaz chopping it up with his father.

"Tiaz, I was really counting on homeboy coming through on that second vest," Melvin said disappointedly.

"Don't wet that second vest, pop. With me watching yo' back out there in the field, won't nothing happen to you...trust."

"You that confident, huh?"

"Yep. I get it from my old man."

"Alright now," he threw playful jabs at his son and he threw a couple back at him.

"Nah, for real though. Them niggaz out there ain't ready for what's about to hit 'em. They ain't ready for Melvin and Tiaz. I'm telling you, pop, we 'bouta be the reason drug dealers and hustlers can't sleep at night. Fools gone be waking up in cold sweats 'cause of us," Tiaz pulled out his Beretta and pointed it at something across the room. "Shiiiiit, as far as I'm concerned, OG, anybody can get it on our road to riches...anybody."

Jerome had just walked out of the house and pulled the door shut. He made his way down the stairs, licking his thumb and counting up the money he'd earned fucking with that nigga Melvin.

*I'ma 'bouta get high. Realllll high and real fast,* Jerome thought to himself.

Unbeknownst to Melvin and Tiaz the crackhead had overheard their conversation. And it was a chance that one day all that they had said would come back to haunt them.

Tranay Adams

## CHAPTER FOURTEEN
### *The next night*

A white man in an overcoat sat inside of Denny's with his apple jack and a Grand Slam before him. He was sure the breakfast was lukewarm seeing as how he'd ordered it twenty minutes ago. Although he'd placed the order he didn't have an appetite. In fact, he'd only gotten the food as to not garner any attention to himself. You see, he was there to meet with someone to make an illegal exchange. A very illegal exchange, if you know what I mean. To be precise, he was there to meet someone that was interested in buying the six bricks of raw cocaine inside of the trunk of his car.

The white man found himself glancing at his watch for the fifteenth time, within that hour, and all it did was make him more anxious than he already was. Figuring that he'd give homeboy he was there to see an extra five minutes, he took a sip of his coffee. Just as he sat the cup down on the saucer, Gary, the man he was there to conduct business with, entered through the double doors of the establishment.

Gary entered the restaurant looking nothing like the coke peddler that he actually was. At the moment, he was dressed up like a complete fucking dork. You know, glasses, plaid shirt, Khakis and dress shoes. He stopped just short of the eating area and pushed his glasses back upon his nose, taking in the full scope of the restaurant. Just as he saw the white man he was there to chop up business with, a waitress approached. They had a brief exchange before Gary pointed over to the man that he was there to see. The waitress glanced in the white man's direction and went about her business, seeing if patrons wanted anything else to go with their respective meals.

The white man rose to his feet to greet Gary. Once the coke peddler reached his table, they shook hands and exchanged pleasantries. Gary then slid into the seat at the booth.

"Sorry about the tardiness, but I couldn't leave the house 'til my wife got home to watch our son." Gary told him.

"Don't worry about it. I know how it can be; I have a couple of kids of my own, three to be exact. They're a handful, which is why my wife and I hired a nanny," the white man replied in a very proper voice.

"Now there's an idea. I may have to consider getting the misses and me one as well."

"I'll advise it. Our Georgette helps us a great deal. Over the years she's become like family," he took a sip of coffee. "Well, I know you didn't come here for my charming personality, so let's get down to business, shall we?"

"My man," Gary smiled and smacked his hand down upon the table top playfully, rattling homeboy's cup of coffee. "That's what I'm talkin' about, let's get the ball rollin'. Show me what chu got." He rubbed his hands together in anticipation. He observed as the white man reached inside of his overcoat and pulled out a small envelope. Looking all around him to make sure that there wasn't anyone watching him; he placed the envelope onto the table top and slid it before Gary. He gave him a nod and watched as he opened the envelope.

"This is some decent shit, right?" Gary asked the man suspiciously, holding the envelope open and staring up at him. He seriously hoped that the white dude had some phenomenal work on his hands because he was in desperate need. His plug had gotten knocked and he was sitting on his last brick. Once that was gone, he didn't know what the fuck he was going to do. So his only hope was to link up with someone that could hit him off with some decent shit to tie him over until he found a plug that could supply him regularly.

"My friend, I could sit here for centuries telling you about how I have the best dope in town, and what have you not. But I'd rather you try my product out for yourself and be the judge, you understand where I'm coming from?"

"Fa sho'," he replied.

Taking his pinky finger, Gary dabbed it into the white powdery substance. Once he had the substance on his pinky finger, he slid it back and forth across his gums and tasted it. Instantly, his gums went numb like they had been shot with nova cane and a smile stretched across his lips. Gary liked the white man. Not only did he have some fire product on his hands, but he didn't brag about it like so many other drug dealers around the city. Gary hated when niggaz talked up their drugs, because once you tried the shit you found out that it was garbage. This was true for most.

"I take it you like what I have to offer, is that safe to say?" The white man asked.

"Oh, yeah, most definitely," Gary folded the envelope up and tucked it into his shirt's pocket.

"Well, I showed you mine, now show me yours."

"Mine is outside in the car," he told him of the money he'd brought along for the exchange.

"Alright then, outside we go," the white man smacked his apple jack back upon his crown and adjusted it to his liking. Right after, the white man pulled out a small fold of money and peeled off a twenty dollar bill, dropping it on the table top. He then motioned for Gary to follow him outside to his car.

\*\*\*

After Gary recovered his backpack from the trunk of his car, he followed the white man to a burgundy old school

Cadillac Deville. Although the vehicle was forty-five years old, it was cleaner than a bitch and drove just as smooth. Stepping to the trunk of the car, the white man unlocked it with his keys. Taking a step back, he lifted the trunk of the Caddy. Gary was startled to see a young man lying in the trunk with a silenced Beretta pointed at his chest. The youngsta wore an orange bandana over his head and the lower half of his face. A pair of black sunglasses concealed his eyes from the world.

"Damn, homie, it's like that?" Gary asked the man that he was interested in buying the kilos from. At that moment, he couldn't believe the luck that he was having. Here he was thinking he was about to purchase some supreme dope and then he finds out it's a mothafucking jack move. *Goddamn it!*

"Just like that, hand it over," the white man, who was really Melvin, scowled and held out his hand for the backpack. He was speaking in his real voice now. Gary exhaled and passed him the backpack reluctantly. Once he confirmed that the money was inside of the backpack, he zipped it back up. "Lie down on your stomach and put your hands behind your head." He ordered Gary with authority.

"Slow yo' roll potnas!" A tall, muscular copper skinned nigga stepped up wearing a doo-rag with the flap over his head. His head whipped from Melvin to Tiaz consistently, daring one of them to make a move so that his toys could act the fuck up. This was Armageddon, Gary's bodyguard and enforcer. His gloved hands clutched a .9mm each and their most dangerous ends were pointed at Melvin and Tiaz. You could tell from the outlining of his shirt that he wore a bulletproof vest underneath his white T-shirt. The dark green ink against his flesh showcased his loved ones names and his gang affiliation. "Drop them bangas, fa I put somethin' hot in y'all bitches heads, man!" He head whipped back and forth between Melvin and Tiaz again. He didn't see any of them making a move to discard their weapons and this pissed him off. He felt that he was the one that had the drop on them so they should have been following his orders. "I suggest y'all hoes do as I said, 'cause I'm not in the habit of repeating myself."

"Son, hand Gary here yo' gun," Melvin told Tiaz. Although he spoke to his boy, he kept his eyes on the threat standing before him.

"Fuck that, pop, if we go down, then we go down squeezing," Tiaz said, swaying his Beretta from Gary to the man with the two guns. They both were anxiously awaiting a reason to bust their guns and leave the other slumped.

"It's alright, son. They have us dead to rights," Melvin stated, never taking his eyes off the two men.

"Yeah, *son*, you heard yo' old man, pass that banga over to my nigga Gary, 'fore I leave both you hoes out here twisted!" Homie with the two 9 Double M's urged him. He was a second away from letting his guns blow holes through niggaz out there, but he was trying to avoid the unnecessary bodies.

"But, pop," Tiaz glanced at his father as he held that Beretta on Gary and homeboy with the two handguns.

"No buts, Junior, you unass your piece…now!" Melvin spoke angrily. This caused Gary to smile harder and wiggle his fingers for the gun that Tiaz had in his possession. Tiaz took a deep breath and handed the banga over to Gary. As soon as the lethal weapon graced his palm a strange sound broke through the air of silence.

*Choot!*

A bullet appeared to have came out of nowhere going through the nigga clutching the two .9mm's forehead. His head snapped back upon impact of the bullet and blood misted the air. He fell backwards, releasing his toys and bumping his head on the curb. *His ass was dead!*

Gary gasped and whipped his head over his shoulder at the nigga he'd brought along to watch his back during the transaction, saying, "Armageddon!"

When Gary whipped his head back around to Melvin, a bullet went through his right eye and out of the back of his skull. He collapsed to the ground and dropped the Beretta. His good eye was wide open and his mouth was ajar. His right eye was blown out; a gaping black hole was there streaming blood.

Tiaz climbed out of the trunk looking all around with confusion. He didn't have an idea as to where the bullet had come from. He thought it must have been a sniper's bullet, but it was just him and his father out there. They didn't have any one else watching their back. That's when he looked to his old man and saw that there was a dummy arm occupying the sleeve of his overcoat. His real arm was actually hidden inside of his coat, aiming a silenced through his coat's pocket. Tiaz smiled behind the bandana. His father was always one step ahead of everything.

"Come on, son, get that backpack so we can get ghost. The police will be here in a minute," Melvin looked around for any witnesses, hearing the police car sirens nearing their location. Once Tiaz snatched up the bag, he slammed the trunk shut and hopped into the front passenger seat. His father slid in behind the wheel and fired up the Caddy, peeling away from the scene.

*** 

Melvin stood before the medicine cabinet's mirror wiping the makeup from off his face from the night's disguise. On the toilet's lid was the wig and mustache he'd wore, which he peeled off not long ago. Once Melvin had finished removing the makeup from off his face and hands he took a shower. After taking care of his hygiene and throwing on underwear, he made his way out of the bathroom. On the bed sat Tiaz, counting up the money that they'd made that night from the jack that they'd laid down. When Tiaz looked up from where he was counting up that money, he saw his father emerging from out of the bathroom. He was rubbing the towel behind his ears and neck. In the background, he saw the bathroom, which was occupied by a hot fog as well as the medicine cabinet's mirror. It was fogged up as well.

"What we looking like, son?" Melvin inquired, sitting down on the opposite side of the bed from his son.

Tiaz was sifting through the money and counting it under his breath. Having heard his father's voice, he looked up at him and held up one finger, signaling for him to give him one minute before he answered. His father obliged him and went about the task of rubbing the wetness from around his neck and ears.

Once Tiaz finished the count, he stacked the bills up neatly and tangled a rubber band around them. He then tossed the stack of money over into a pile where he had the rest of the money.

"That's ninety racks, pop." Tiaz told his old man, pulling an ink pen from behind his ear and grabbing the small black book from off the nightstand. Inside of this book was all of the money they'd robbed and killed for. Every last dollar of the blood money was scribbled down inside of the little black book with the brass lock on it.

"Ninety G's from this last lick?" Melvin frowned up as he continued to rub the wetness from himself. "You pay that nigga Nathadious off?"

Tiaz stopped jotting in the little black book and said, "Yeah, I went to pay 'em off, pop."

"You went to pay 'em off? What happened?" Melvin questioned with concern.

*Nathadious sat behind the wheel of his Buick LaSabre taking the occasional pull of his stinky cigar. His big black lips sucked on the end of the overgrown cancer stick and the ember tip of it glowed. Smoke wafted from out of his nostrils and he rolled a thick fog from off of his tongue. The entire time he indulged in the tobacco, he listened to an old B.B King song, The Thrill Is Gone. After taking one more pull from the end of his cheap cigar, he took it from his lips and played an imaginary guitar along with the man himself, eyelids shut. He was jamming. He was jamming like he was B.B King himself, sitting down on stage in front of a sold out audience of his adoring fans.*

*The thrill is gone*
*The thrill is gone away*
*The thrill is gone, baby*
*The thrill is gone away*
*You know you done me wrong baby*
*And you'll be sorry someday*
*Knock! Knock! Knock!*

*A loud rap at the passenger window startled Nathadious and he went to grab his gun from underneath the seat. Right when he'd raised his gun, he looked up to see Tiaz at the window.*

*"You slow, OG. A young nigga coulda been done bucked you down by the time you grabbed yo' heat. Open up, man," Tiaz clutched the door handle and waited for Nathadious to let him in.*

*"Young blood, you damn near made me have a heart attack," he opened the door and slid his gun back underneath the seat where he'd gotten it. He then settled back in his seat, looking over at Tiaz as he opened the door and slid inside on the leather interior. Nathadious had his greedy eyes on the bowling bag that the young nigga was toting the entire time. He licked his lips hungrily when he*

seen it. Tiaz didn't even have to say it. His cut for putting them on to the lick was definitely stored inside of it.

"My bad, my nigga, I wasn't tryna scare you or no shit. Hopefully, what I got here in this bag will ease some of that tension for you," Tiaz smiled and patted the leather bowling bag.

"Oh, I'm sure it will," Nathadious looked at the bag in anticipation, rubbing his hands together. He reached over and unzipped the bowling bag while it sat in Tiaz' lap. His brows furrowed when he didn't see anything but darkness. That's when his head snapped up and he met Tiaz' scowling face. Right then, his eyes bugged and he gasped.

Blocka!

Blood speckled Tiaz' face as he squeezed his eyelids shut. Half of Nathadious's head exploded upon impact of the slug, launching his skull backwards. His dome banged up against the driver side window which was already splattered with his blood. His head turned to the side, displaying his bulged eyes and wide opened mouth. He expired with terror etched across his chubby, hairy face.

"Argh! Fuck!" Tiaz squeezed his eyelids harder and gritted his teeth, pressing his finger inside of his ear. His eyelids snapped back open, hearing the strange reoccurring siren in both of his eardrums. He didn't know that firing his gun in such close quarters would cause him such pain. He was suffering for it now, but it was a lesson learned. "Fat mothafucka!" The young nigga pulled his hand, which was clutching a Glock, free from out of the opening he'd cut inside of the bowling bag. He flung open the car door and fell out onto the ground, dropping the bag. The shot that rang out inside of the confines of the vehicle had disturbed his equilibrium. Having struggled to get back upon his feet, he slammed the passenger door shut and wiped the specks of blood from off his face with the back of his hand. Looking up, he was just in time to see

*Threat pulling up in his grandmother's Cadillac. As soon as he stopped beside him, Tiaz ran around the car and hopped into the front passenger seat. Afterwards, he slammed the door shut and ordered him to drive off. As he sped off, Tiaz continued to squeeze his eyelids shut and grit his teeth, holding his fingers inside of his ears to block out the strange siren.*

"Nigga was shot dead when I got to the meeting place, so I fell back and kept the money," Tiaz lied with a straight face.

"Damn, you never know when the Grim Reaper will come knocking at cha door," Melvin shook his head. He felt like it was a goddamn shame that someone had murdered Nathadious.

"You ain't never lied, OG," Tiaz gathered up the money and stored it inside of a safe at the back of the closet. He then rose to his feet and walked back over to the bed, picking up the overcoat that his father had sewn the dummy arm into. He turned the overcoat from front to back, examining it carefully. He had to admit to himself that his old man was pretty clever having come up with an idea like that one.

## CHAPTER FIFTEEN

Three months later, Melvin and Tiaz had robbed everyone from corner hustlers to neighborhood dopemen since they started getting money the ski mask way. In no time they had stacked up more money than they could ever dream of sticking niggaz up. They set hoods on fire with their exploits, leaving niggaz shaking in their boots and the streets gossiping about their get down.

With the streets being as hot as a firecracker, Melvin and Tiaz decided to take a one month hiatus to let things cool off. Although Tiaz wanted to keep getting money, Melvin wasn't having it. He knew that it was in their best interest to fallback because the greedy got caught and football numbers.

Melvin sat at the bar hunched over a glass of something dark. After he took a sip of his alcohol beverage, he looked at the glass and hissed, feeling the liquid fire engulf his belly. The liquor was as strong as a donkey's hind legs, but it was well needed with the way he was feeling, which was depressed. Although most people may have felt that everyday above ground was a good day, he wasn't so sure that he felt the same, especially since he didn't have his wife to live his life with. Besides his son, there wasn't anything he had worth living for. In fact, it hurt him immensely every morning and night that he woke up or laid down, realizing that his wife wasn't lying beside him.

A life without Kimberly wasn't a life to him at all. He desperately yearned to be in her presence. And it killed him to know that, that day may not be coming any time soon. No matter how badly he wanted it.

Melvin downed the last of his drink and held up his glass. "Nigel," Melvin called out the bartender's name. He came walking over cleaning out a beer mug with a rag.

"Another?" Nigel asked.

"Yep."

"Coming up," the bartender headed off to pour up the drink that the patron requested.

When he left, Melvin looked around the establishment; everyone was either shooting pool or enjoying conversation over cold beers. Seeing someone approaching through his peripherials, he turned around to see Chief coming from around the corner, where the hallway and pay phones were located.

Melvin recalled seeing the stocky bald head dude on his way to the men's room. He slowed his walking to ease drop on his conversation. In doing so, he overheard him talking about a cat that had been banging his wife, and how he'd pay good money to have him knocked off.

"What can I get for you, Chief?" Nigel approached the stocky bald head man that had just sat at the bar beside Melvin.

"The usual," Chief grabbed a few of the cashews out of the bowl on the bar top and threw them back. Munching on them, he took a look at the establishment. While he was taking in the full scope of the scenary, Nigel was coming back with the drink he'd made for him. He sat a napkin down and sat the glass down on top of it.

Hearing someone at his rear, Chief spun around on the stool to find his drink waiting for him. He thanked the bartender and indulged in his alcohol beverage.

"Hey, how you doing? Dewayne. Dewayne Chapman," Melvin outstretched his hand in greeting.

Chief's brows furrowed. He didn't know what the man was being so friendly for. He was hesitant to shake his hand as he wondered if he was friend or foe, so he ran his face and name through his mental database. When he didn't come up with any beef associated with either, he reluctantly shook his hand, firmly.

"Chief. Chief Jackson," he introduced himself, giving him his government name.

"Pleasure to meet chu."

Chief nodded and said, "Look here, Dewayne, your notta faggot, are you? If so, you may as well keep that shit moving some where over there. I like pussy, that's it."

Melvin chuckled. "Nah, homie, I'm not gay. I just figured maybe I could help you with your problem."

"Problem?" He raised an eyebrow. "Who says I have a problem?"

"You did. I overheard you on the phone."

"You're a nosey mothafucka, bruh. I ain't got no problem," he stated sternly and turned back around to the bar, taking a sip from his glass.

"I'm sorry, I guess I was mistaken. I apologize, have a nice night," Melvin rose from the bar stool. Next, he paid for his drinks and dropped the bartender a tip on the bar top. He then grabbed his overcoat and Dub hat, adjusting it on his head. He then held up his fist in salute to Nigel and went on about his business, heading for the exit.

As Melvin strolled toward the door, Chief took the time out to think to himself and take another sip of his drink.

*Maybe ol' boy was the real deal? A hitta would be the perfect solution to my situation right now. He could pop that nigga J-Murda and I'll have 'em outta my hair for good. But on the other hand, what if this dude is One Time, looking to snatch my black ass up? I ain't tryna go to jail, man, fuck! A nigga ain't tryna get locked up,* Chief thought to himself, rubbing his hand down his shaved head. He then shut his eyelids and massaged the bridge of his nose, licking his lips. If he was going to make a decision then he had to make one now before the man that could help him out of his situation was out of the door and gone forever.

*Fuck it! I gotta take a chance and roll the dice.*

"Ayo, my man," Chief called out across the bar.

Chief's words froze Melvin at the exit with his back to him. He couldn't see it, but Melvin was smiling from ear to ear. He quickly checked himself and brought his fist to his mouth, clearing his throat. Afterwards, he turned around to the man he was talking to last at the bar.

"What's up?" Melvin inquired.

"You gotta minute?"

Melvin pulled back the sleeve of his overcoat and looked at his watch. He was fronting like he didn't have much time, but that was bullshit. He really didn't have shit to do that night. All he planned on doing was ordering takeout and watching reruns of *Different Strokes*. See, he just wanted homie to believe he was a man that always had something going. Therefore, he had very little time. That was the impression that he wanted to project.

"Yeah, I gotta few ticks," Melvin made his way back over to the bar and sat down where he was before, beside Chief.

"Jack, right?" Chief asked of Melvin's drink of choice. He'd noticed earlier that night that the man had ordered up a glass of Jack Daniel's straight. He believed that homie must have had a cast iron belly to keep such strong liquor down because he didn't know anyone that could handle that kind of alcohol without a chaser.

"You got it."

In no time Nigel was back with Melvin's drink of choice. He placed a napkin down and placed the glass of Jack down on top of it. Afterwards, he went about his duty of wiping down the bar top to leave the two men to their conversation.

"First off, are you Five Owe?" Chief asked in a hushed tone.

"Nah, I ain't no pig," he chuckled and then took a sip of his drink.

"You know if you are you gotta tell me, right? Or it's entrapment."

"Well, I'm telling you right now, I ain't the fucking cops."

Chief's eyes glanced at something across the bar and then they landed back on Melvin. He blew out his frustration in the form of a hot breath before going on, "Okay, alright. There's this young nigga I need to be made a memory..." he cut himself short once Melvin lifted his hand and looked around, trying to make sure that no one had overheard him since he was speaking a little too loud. Once he saw that no one inside of the establishment was paying any attention to them. He told him to lower his voice and to proceed with what he had to say. "Like I was saying, there's this young nigga I need to be made a memory. Son of a bitch has been running dick up in my wife, bastard done fucked around and knocked her up at that."

"Lemme guess, you want me to do them both?"

"Nah, it's just him for now. Like I said, my wife is pregnant. Now, I don't know if it's mine yet. If I find out that the kid is not mine then I guess you and I will be having this conversation again in the next couple of weeks."

"What if you find out that the baby is yours?"

"Then wifey and I are gonna try to make this family thang work."

*Damn, that bitch should be on her knees praying to God right now 'cause homeboy gone for sho' drop the bag to get her ass cleaned up if that kid isn't his,* Melvin thought to himself and then indulged in his drink.

"I hear you."

"Fucking bitch, man, I'ma chef and got my own lil' business. I'm doing lovely. I take good care of her, treat her like she's fucking royalty, only to find out that she giving my pussy to some street nigga, young enough to be my fucking nephew. I tell you, man, these bitches are so ungrateful. You give 'em the moon and they'll complain about not having the goddamn stars to go with it." Chief went on rambling like Melvin wasn't even there. He sat his drink down on the bar top and directed his attention to the man that wanted to try his hand at contract killing.

*Fuck didn't he just tell his wife to stop fucking with the young head? He could save himself a lotta money. I'm curious, but I'm not 'bouta ask 'em and fuck around and talk myself outta some paypa.*

"I know what you're thinking," Chief began. "Why don't I just have my wife stop fucking with 'em, right? Well, I tried that approach and the lil' mothafucka threatened to kill me if she cut 'em off."

"You read my mind," Melvin drunk the rest of his alcohol and sat the glass down. It tripped him out how Chief told him what he was thinking. It was like he was a psychic or some shit like that.

"Now, how much is it gonna run me to send this lil' gangbanging ass nigga on this vacation to Satan's house?" He finished off his drink and sat the glass down as well.

"Twenty-five grand...half up front," he told him with dead serious eyes.

"Jesus, twenty-five stacks? What're you saving up for early retirement?"

"Shouldn't we all be?"

"You goddamn right we should, lemme pay for this drink and we'll finish this conversation outside," he rose from off his stool and dropped a few dollars on the bar top. He then smacked his hat on his head and threw up his hand, bidding Nigel a farewell. Afterwards, he headed out of the establishment with Melvin on his heels.

Melvin and Chief walked down the sidewalk with their hands in their pockets, talking in hushed tones about the business that they had on the table.

"I can get chu that upfront money by tomorrow night. The other half, I'll slide that to you once the job is done. Is that all right by you?"

"That's perfectly fine."

"Great."

"Here's what I'm gonna need from," Melvin began, "A photograph of this fool, and any information on places that he frequents."

"Places that he frequents?" He raised an eyebrow.

"Yes. I know you wouldn't want me laying homeboy down anywhere around yo' house, now would you? Trust me, that shit would look realllll suspicious seeing as how I'm sure your next door neighbors have seen this dude running in and out of your home. You can't tell me that they haven't put two and two together and figured out that the misses is serving him slices of that good old putang pie. If you know what I mean," he nudged him and gave him a look that said *You know your neighbors know your wife is banging homeboy.*

"You're right," Chief nodded in agreement. "The next time he comes over to the house I'll have my old lady snap some pictures of 'em, or I can hide somewhere and get 'em myself. As far as the places he frequents, I'll have to ask Janella about that. I'm sure she knows something. She's been banging his lil' young ass behind my back for the past five years, that fucking whore," he balled his hand into a fist and clenched it tightly, causing veins to form in it. He then gritted his teeth and his eyebrows arched, nose scrunching up. His wife had hurt him bad by fucking around on him, but he still loved her. That was one of the reasons why he was going to try to make things work between them. He just hoped and prayed that the baby she was carrying was his, because if it wasn't, then he was going to be taking out a contract with Melvin on her ass too. He couldn't see himself raising his woman's side nigga'z baby; he'd look like a goddamn fool. *No way no how! Fuck that!* "You gotta light, bruh?" He asked as he reached inside of his overcoat and pulled out a pack of Newport 100s, smacking the bottom of the pack in his palm.

"Yeah, I got one here somewhere." Melvin fished around inside of his pockets and then patted himself down. Feeling a small rectangle shaped bulge inside of his overcoat, he reached inside and pulled out his lighter. He then took the liberty of lighting the tip of his client's cigarette, watching him suck on the end of it and blow out a cloud of smoke.

"Where do you want me to drop the bag off to you?" Chief asked as he continued to walk beside Melvin, taking casual puffs of his Joe.

"The Bar Fly…meet me here on Thursday. That's two days from now," he told him. "Be here sayyyyyy eight o'clock?" He looked at Chief to confirm the drop off location.

"Thursday night at eight, it is." Chief stopped and turned to Melvin and shook his hand firmly.

\*\*\*

"This of 'em, pop, this one of them niggaz!" Tiaz tapped his Beretta against one of the many photos of J-Murda he held in his hand. Chief had met up with Melvin to drop off the bag for the kill and the photographs so he'd know what his prey looked like. As soon as Melvin got home he showed his son the money and the photos he was given.

"One of the niggaz that what?" Melvin's forehead wrinkled. He didn't have a clue of what his son was talking about.

"One of the niggaz that packed me and Threat out in that alley," Tiaz sat the photo down upon the table top before his father and he picked it up. Melvin looked over the photo with a concentrated expression fixed on his face. He then looked up at son and said, "Are you sure this is him?"

"Positive. I'll never forget that mothafucka'z face...never," he paced back and forth across the kitchen floor looking at the photograph with his gun down at his side, pressing its red safety button *on* and *off*. "I'ma roll witchu on this fa sho'," he handed his father the photograph back and he continued to look over it. "I gotta be the nigga to push his hairline back. You feel me?"

"I got cha, son," Melvin nodded and pulled his son in under his arm. "And don't worry; he's all yours once we're on 'em."

"Good looking out, OG." Tiaz dapped up his father.

"No problem," Melvin sat the photograph down on the table top and sat on the edge of it. "Listen, I was thinking, when we go to hit this fool we should be dressed up as the other side just in case somebody sees us out there. Besides, it wouldn't be such a bad idea to cover our asses, ya never know."

"You got it, pop." He dapped up his old man again.

Money was the motive.

Tranay Adams

## CHAPTER SIXTEEN

Melvin and Tiaz followed J-Murda from his house in Norwalk to a party on 65th and Gramercy. When they got there, Melvin parked eight cars down the street from the olive green house that the party was taking place. He and Tiaz were slumped in the seats of a stolen '83 Buick Regal, their getaway car. Tiaz had stolen the vehicle himself and replaced the license plates in case the cops tailed them and decided to check the placard.

Melvin and Tiaz were dressed in black from head to toe. Tiaz had on a hoodie, red bandana, red Dickie's and All Star Chuck Taylor Converses. Melvin donned a beanie, a red bandana, black jean jacket and boots. Melvin gripped a Beretta and so did his son. So far the pair had spent a total of four hours staking out the olive green house waiting for J-Murda to make his exit. Tiaz had grown impatient, and all of his bitching and complaining was getting on his father's nerves.

"Damn, pop, this nigga taking a long as time," Tiaz complained from the front passenger seat. "I wish he'd show his face so I can blow that bitch off and get it over with. I'm tryna collect that bag," he said, clicking the safety button *on* and *off* his Beretta.

"Son, you are some kind of impatient, you know that?" Melvin looked to his son smirking. "You gotta fallback and stay calm. We'll get 'em, all we gotta do is wait for 'em. Trust me, he'll come out. And as soon as he does you'll get your chance. I promise you that."

"You right, pop."

"I know I'm right. With age comes mistakes and lessons learned. Experience is the best teacher. Niggaz can't tell you about shit that they never been through. Most will try, but few will listen. You know why? 'Cause people aren't trying to listen to a mothafucka that ain't never treaded through the waters that they have. You feel me?"

Tiaz smiled and said, "I feel you, pop. That's why you my OG. I fucks witchu."

"I fucks witchu too, junior," he focused his attention back on the windshield, watching the house that J-Murda went inside of.

"I'm for real OG. You not just my pop's, you my rider, my homie and my nigga, I love you," he dapped up his old man.

"I appreciate that, son. I feel the same about chu."

"Pop, can I ask you a question?" When he asked this, he found his father pulling back his sleeve and looking at his watch, frown fixed on his face.

"Sure, son, shoot," he sat up in his seat and focused his eyes on the house that they were staked out of.

"Not to get all mushy and shit. But I gotta ask, how come every time I tell you I love you, you never say it back? I mean, I know you do, but I gotta admit. Sometimes it would be nice to…"

"Shhh," Melvin hushed Tiaz, holding his finger to his lips. "I think that's him," he nodded to the windshield at J-Murda. He'd just exited the house party with a cute little brown skinned number under his arm.

"Yeah, that's his bitch ass," Tiaz' eyebrows sloped and wrinkles formed across the beginning of his nose. He clenched his jaws and showcased the muscles in his face. Unbeknownst to him, he'd gripped his Beretta tightly. He wanted that mothafucka J-Murda bad. In fact, he couldn't wait to open up his face with a magazine of some hot shit. "I'll never forget that dick sucka's face for as long as I breathe! And I'ma make sure my face is the last one he sees before I give him his tombstone. That's on the gang!" Tiaz went on to check the magazine of his gun. He'd done so before he brought the weapon along, but he wanted to be extra sure. The last thing he wanted was to not have enough bullets to finish the job that he came to do. Nah, once he started firing, he wasn't going to let up until he was sure his enemy's cripping days were over. Straight up!

"Alright, son, here he comes. It's time to move." Melvin pulled his bandana up over the lower half of his face so that it would be covering his nose and mouth. Looking to his son, he gave him a nod and then he opened his door. He jumped out on his bending knees and held the door open, allowing his son to come out right behind him. Once Tiaz had vacated the vehicle, Melvin shut the door as quietly as he could. He then gave his offspring the signal to follow him. Together, hunched over, they made their way around their car and headed towards the house that J-Murda had just left.

\*\*\*

J-Murda emerged from the olive green house well under the influence of the drugs and alcohol that were the party favors at the function. He was fucked up, but not as fucked up as homegirl under his right arm. She was pissy drunk and trying to walk with legs of spaghetti.

Although J-Murda was high, his dick was fully functional. As his eyes toured every inch of the cutie under his arm, all he could think about was blowing her back out. He wanted to hit her raw, too, even though he knew he shouldn't with all the diseases that were going around today. He kept having flashes of the brown skinned girl gagging on the end of his dick while he mouth fucked her. His hardness bulged in the crotch of his navy blue Dickie shorts as he rolled the thought over and over in his head. He couldn't have fucked her in the house because the homies had every bedroom in that bitch sewn up with a broad of their own. And he was too horny to wait until he got her back to his place or a nearby motel. So he led her drunken ass over into the rose bushes in front of the house. With the stature of the bushes and it being dark out, the young nigga had enough cover for them to get busy.

J-Murda bent homegirl over and held her purple thong away from her bald pussy. Taking his tattooed freehand, he dipped into his Dickie shorts and withdrew his grown man. He spat a glob of saliva into his palm and lubed up his meat. Brown skin hissed and tensed up as the hoodsta split her walls apart with his third leg. J-murda buckled a little feeling the hood rat's warm, wetness. A smile broadened his face and he licked his lips. He then tilted his head back and shut his eyelids.

"Oh, my damn," J-Murda said under his breath. "Cuz, this shit fiyah," he spoke on how bomb her pussy was to him.

J-Murda grabbed a lock of brown skin's hair and pulled her head back, drawing a soft whine from her full lips. While his left hand held tight to her hair, his right hand cupped her right breast. He grunted like a guerilla as he fucked her from behind. Moans of pleasure and pain escaped brown skin's lips as the hoodsta banged her out. His pummeling her from the back sent ripples up her buttocks. She had never been fucked like this before, and homeboy was laying the pipe down with a capital D. He had her ass with her eyelids squeezed shut, moaning, groaning and speaking in tongues.

Seeing something moving in his peripherals, J-Murda turned to his left and found two dark figures ascending from the shadows, and moving in on the yard. Feeling death closing in on him made him sober up quickly. He reached for the .38 in his waistline and grabbed air. That's when he realized he had dropped it in the bushes while he and little momma were freaking off. J-Murda felt around in the bushes trying to find his strap in the dark. Brown skin saw the smaller of the two figures invade the yard and she screamed in hysterics. The last thing she saw was flickers of fire in the dark figure's outstretched hand before her chest exploded into a mass of crimson.

As soon as J-Murda picked up his strap, he felt a sharp pain in the meat of his left butt cheek. That's when it dawned on him that he had been shot. Gun arm erect, J-Murda turned around and was greeted with a chest full of hot lead. He fell back against the house and slid down to the ground, leaving a smear of blood behind him. J-Murda lay slumped up against the house, coughing up blood. His sight was blurring and he felt himself fading into the next life.

The smallest of the dark figures stood over him victorious. He pulled his bandana down from the lower half of his face to reveal his identity. J-Murda vision came in and out of focus. It registered that in his mind that it was Tiaz and a taller man standing over him.

"Ah, shit!" J-Murda managed to say with a mouthful of blood. He knew that this was definitely the end for him. He recalled what had happened in the alley that night and knew that the youngsta wasn't about to leave the killing field without his life.

"*Ah, shit*, is right!" Tiaz told him as he stared down upon him with murder in his eyes. His eyebrows were arched and his nose was scrunched up.

J-Murda laughed manically and said, "I'll see you in hell," he then threw up his hood one last time.

"Take these with you!" Tiaz spat with extreme prejudice. He pulled the trigger of his weapon and it bucked in his hand. Empty shell casings flew from it as flames ignited its silenced barrel. J-Murda's dome burst like a rotten pumpkin. There was no way his ass would get an open casket funeral now. The sight before Tiaz' eyes brought him great pleasure. It was like 2pac said *Revenge was like the sweetest joy next to getting pussy.*

"Bitch ass, faggot ass nigga! Fuck you and yo' dead homies!" Tiaz spat some more fire at him just cause.

Melvin placed his hand on his son's shoulder while looking down at the corpse he'd just created. "Come on, son, let's go."

"Hold up, pop," Tiaz pulled the bandana back over the lower half of his face and kneeled down to J-Murda, whose eyes were staring out of their corners at nothing. His mouth was wide open and his tongue was visible. "We need something to confirm our kill," he snatched the Cuban link gold chain from around his neck which was holding onto the dead man's name, J-Murda. The gold and crushed diamond piece was stained with blood. The blood on the piece made its diamonds look like rubies.

Tiaz stood up and looped J-Murda's chain around his neck. He turned to walk back to the getaway car with his father and all hell broke loose.

The front door of the house swung open and an army of thug ass niggaz came pouring out. All Tiaz and Melvin saw, besides mean mugs, were close fades, cornrows, tattoos and gang banga attire. There wasn't a soul amongst the cavalry that didn't bare a gun of his or her own.

"Go for the car!" Melvin called out to his son as he opened fire on the engaging crips, trying to lay some cover for his son. Tiaz ran from out of the yard, firing his Beretta as he retreated for the vehicle. One of the crips took a hot one to the chest and crumpled like a brown paper bag. Another one took a bullet to the thigh and abdomen; he tumbled down the steps and onto the pavement, screaming like a little bitch.

"Ahhhh, fuck, cuz, its hot! These fucking bullets are hot!" He cried out as he held his bleeding torso. His shirt turned burgundy from his blood absorbing it.

Tiaz cleared the threshold of the yard with Melvin following close behind. Slowing to stop, Melvin turned around and let off two shots: the first bullet whizzed past one of the crips' heads, while the other struck one in the neck. The nigga hollered out and smacked his hand over the squirting hole in his neck as he squeezed his eyelids shut. Melvin had turned back around, and was on his way out of the yard, when a crip in a Mariners' fitted cap ran to the bottom of the steps and kneeled down on one knee. Clutching his handgun in both hands, the hoodsta closed his right eye and took aim. You could tell by the way he held his gun and positioned his self, that he wasn't an amateur shooter. He had to have had a couple of bodies under his belt.

Mariners fitted cap cracked off two rounds. The bullets ripped through the air coming at Melvin in what appeared to be slow motion to Tiaz. His eyes widen with fear seeing that his father was in grave danger because he wasn't wearing a bulletproof vest. Through all the chaos the only thing that Tiaz could see were those copper bullets. Everything else was blurry and in black and white to him. He didn't even hear anything, it was silence.

Haa! Haa! Haa! Haa!" Tiaz breathed huskily, running as fast as he could to reach his father. He jumped on top of the short gate and leaped off of it, sailing across the air. He launched his body across his father's back which was where the life threatening bullets were headed, "Aaahhhhh!" He hollered out in pain and squeezed his eyelids into slits. The bullets ripped his clothing into shreds and embedded into his bulletproof vest.

Tiaz wasn't the nigga that the dude in the Mariners fitted cap intended on popping, but he was just as good. Seeing that he had one of his homeboy's executioners down, he gripped his weapon tighter and aimed it right between Tiaz' eyes.

"Get the fuck away from my boy!" A vengeful cry ripped through the night's air.

Mariners fitted cap was just about to deliver the kill shot when bullets flew out of nowhere tatting his chest up. He did a little dance and collapsed to the ground. His fitted cap landed not too far away from him.

Tiaz looked out of the yard and saw his father. He was leaned over the rooftop of the idling getaway car with his smoking Beretta pointed in the dead crip's direction. He had been the one that laid old boy down and saved his life.

"Come on, son," Melvin told him as he continued to fire on the few crips that were left. He was keeping them at bay so that Tiaz could getaway.

Tiaz scrambled to his feet and ran out of the yard with his arm stretched across his body. His ribcage was aching since he'd been shot. He wasn't for sure, but something told him that a couple of his ribs were broken.

Once Tiaz had hopped into the front passenger seat and slammed the door shut, Melvin hopped in behind the wheel and pulled off. Bullets tatted up the side of the Regal and shattered its back window. Tiaz stuck his Beretta out of the window and ripped off shot after shot until his gun was empty.

*Vrooooom!*

The Regal ripped up the block and left debris in its wake. Melvin glanced up at the rearview mirror and saw a couple of crips run out into the middle of the residential street. They pointed their guns at the back of the fleeing car and opened fire. Bullets pinged off the bumper of the getaway car, puncturing its trunk with several holes. This caused Melvin to duck down further and mashe the gas pedal further, accelerating the vehicle's speed. The engine of the car growled as it ripped further up the street. It got so far that the crips appeared as dots through the shattered back window.

"I think...I think the coast is clear, pop." Tiaz said in pain where he was slumped down in the seat. He'd gotten down when the shots came just like his father had.

Melvin slowly rose up in the driver's seat and adjusted the rearview mirror, looking through it. He didn't see any more of the crips. They'd gotten a long way from the house that they'd laid the murder down at.

"How you feeling, junior?" Melvin asked his son. He glanced back and forth between him and the windshield.

"My side is killing me, but I think I'll be straight."

"Lemme see," Melvin unstrapped the left side of his son's bulletproof vest while he unstrapped the other. He then lifted the front of the vest up. He frowned when he saw the bad bruising on his son's ribcage. "I think your ribs may be broken, I'ma call a doctor friend of mine up and see about him coming through the house to check you out."

"Okay. Thanks, pop," he gritted his teeth in pain.

"Thanks for what?" Melvin frowned. He didn't know what his son was talking about.

"Saving my life back there."

"No thanks needed. You're my son and we're partners. We suppose to have one another's back, right?"

"Right."

Tranay Adams

## CHAPTER SEVENTEEN

"Alright," Doc said. He'd just finished putting ointment on Tiaz' bruises and wrapped bandages around his torso. The youngsta's injuries weren't as bad as Melvin had thought. He'd be okay. All he needed was a few days to heal up and he could get back in the game. Melvin already knew better though. There wasn't going to be any down time for his son. No, sir, he was going to be ready to get back into the thick of things ASAP. "You're all set."

"What's up with them pain killers though?" Tiaz said as he brought his arm down from the old doctor wrapping up his torso. He winced feeling the pain from being shot. Although the Kevlar vest he was wearing stopped the bullets, he was still feeling the consequences of being shot.

"Oh, yeah, I almost forgot," Doc grabbed his brown leather bag from off the kitchen table that looked like a bowling bag and unzipped it. Reaching inside, he pulled out an orange pill bottle and tossed it over to the young nigga, who quickly popped the seal and downed four of them. He then turned on the faucet and let warm water fill his palm to wash the pills down. Shutting his eyelids, he threw his head back and swallowed the pills, his throat rolling up and down his neck.

"Take it easy there, cowboy," Doc reacted to Tiaz throwing back so many pills at once. "That's Zydone, shit is addictive. The dosage is on the bottle there." He motioned for Tiaz to turn the pill bottle over. "Fuck around and be staggering around like those zombies outside." He stated, referring to the crackheads that were wandering throughout the hood at night.

"Fuck that!" Tiaz said. "My mothafucking chest is killing me."

"You act as if you haven't been shot before," Melvin said to him from where he was leaning up against the kitchen counter with his arms folded across his chest.

"Aye, you can have your nuts stomped for the $2^{nd}$ time, that doesn't mean you'll ever get used to it, now does it, pop?"

"Can't argue with that logic," Doc interjected, storing his things away inside of his brown leather bag and closing it. When he turned around he saw Melvin reach into his pocket and pull out a roll of $100 dollar bills. He was just about to peel off a few Benjamin and pass them to the doctor until he put his hand up, stopping him.

Doc motioned Melvin over and he stepped before him. The doctor leaned closer to him and spoke in a hushed tone so that Tiaz wouldn't hear what was being said. "I was thinking maybe you could, you know..." he thumbed his nose and sniffed, "hook a brotha up with a little something, something."

"You play witcho nose now? I thought chu was still fucking with the weed," Melvin inquired. See, Melvin's side hustle had always been weed. In addition to being a cab driver and a security guard. He was also the weed man. Quiet as it was kept; he met the good doctor at a party over on the West side by Dominguez University. He use to serve him and his little fraternity brothers ounces of weed. Back then he knew that Doc was going to make PHD because he was on his studies, so he made sure to keep in touch with him. This was because he knew that one day that this plug would come in handy. He was right because here he was, standing inside of his kitchen with the nigga now. "When you start fucking around with coke?"

"Ah, nah, it's not for me," Doc lied. "It's for some colleagues of mine. They're supposed to have some big pool party over in Malibu. You know these rich white folks love to fuck with the nose candy." He smiled and nudged him like he knew exactly what he was talking about.

"Unh huh," Melvin responded, giving him the side eye. He gave him a look like, *Nigga, if you don't knock it off with that bullshit.*

"I'm serious, man. Come on now, you know me for like, forever. Only thing I ever fucked with was weed."

"Say, bruh, ain't no judgment here. I don't really fuck with powder like that, so you'll have to give me a minute," Melvin told him. "You wanna relax in the living room while I make a few calls and see what a couple of partners of mine may have on deck? Otherwise, all I got to offer you is a couple of zips or cold cash for yo' services."

"Damn, man, I sure hate to hear that. I was really looking forward to getting my hands on some white girl. These people are really counting on me to come through for 'em," he looked to the floor and placed his hand on his hip. Holding his bag at his side, he licked his lips and thought about someone else he could probably holler at to get his hands on the drugs that he needed.

"How much of it you looking to get your hands on?" Tiaz butted into the conversation. He'd just slipped his wife beater over his head and straightened it out.

"A couple of ounces, youngsta, hell, about four would do me just fine."

"That's one-hundred and twelve grams. I can fade that," Tiaz told him. "How much you charging for this job you did?"

"I tell you what, lemme pay you for two of those ounces and we're square."

"It's a done deal, homeboy," Tiaz shook the good doctor's hand and went off to retrieve the drugs. He gave the doctor the narcotics when he returned and he paid him for two of them like he promised. The doctor then stashed the drugs inside of his bag and zipped it back up, grabbing it by its handles.

"Gentlemen, it's been a pleasure," Doc shook hands with Melvin and Tiaz. "Lemme gone and get out of here before my wife starts blowing up my phone."

"Alright, I'll see you out to yo' car." Melvin told him.

"No need, Mel. I'm good. I took precautions," he flashed him the holstered pistol on his hip "Mines is registered. I gotta license to kill, nigga. You better ask somebody." He smiled and winked at him as he continued out of the door.

Melvin cracked a grin and saw the doctor to the front door, locking it behind him.

"Boy, aren't chu full of surprises. Now, where in the hell did you score that cocaine from?" Melvin asked his son as he returned to the kitchen.

"That's what I got off a lil' lick me and Threat did some time back."

Melvin nodded his head as he received the news and sat down at the table, across from his son. He watched as he counted up the money the doctor paid him with as he began talking to him.

"I been thinking, maybe it's about time we hang up our guns."

When he said this, Tiaz stopped counting the money and sat it down on the table. A serious expression went across his face as he stared his father in the face.

"Now, why would we do that? We been running up one hell of a check on our run, pop. Remember when them ends wasn't meeting and we were starving about to get thrown out on our asses? Well, I don't know if you have noticed, but the ends our meeting like a mothafucka now," he went back to counting his money and listening to his father.

"I hear you, and we have had a hell of a run. We made a hell of a lotta money too, enough to move outta the ghetto and get ourselves a house in a better place. I'm talking about a place far better than the slum that we live in. We could open up our own business, wash our money and live life legitimately. I'm talking about a life where we wouldn't have to worry about watching over our shoulders for the law or some dope boy coming back for revenge. You know what I'm saying, son?"

"I feel what chu saying, pop," Tiaz claimed. "But I'm not ready to leave the hood, this is all I know. Why is it that every time black people get some money they wanna leave the hood, huh? It's been good enough for us all this time. Now all of a sudden it's not 'cause niggaz gotta lil' money? Besides, we ain't nearly made enough paypa yet. When we get some life changing money, then let's chop it about us stopping."

"Come here, son, I wanna show you something," he motioned for his son to follow him as he headed out of the kitchen.

Tiaz and Melvin entered the master bedroom. Melvin opened the closet door and pulled the drawstring. There was a click sound and a light shined brightly inside of the small space. Melvin moved the few clothes hanging on the rack inside and exposed a black safe. He opened it and revealed stacks and stacks of money inside. The safe was nearly full of money. Reaching inside of the safe, Melvin pulled out the black book that they recorded all of the money they made in. He unlocked the brass lock that sealed the black book shut and opened it. Licking his thumb, he flipped through the pages until he found the page that he was looking for. Turning to his son, he motioned him over and showed him the book. Using his finger, he pointed to the amount they made out in the streets jacking and killing. In total they had made $538,000 dollars in cash.

Tiaz looked surprised seeing that he and his old man had run up racks like that. Now, he knew that they had run some checks up, but never did he figure that they had made that dollar amount.

"Pop, don't play with me," Tiaz said. He couldn't believe that they had really made that much money. "How much did we really make in these streets. Seriously though, don't lie."

Melvin shut the book and locked it, looking at his son, he said, "Long as you've known yo' father, has he ever lied to you about anything?" He spoke of himself in third person.

"No," he had to admit.

"That's right. I been keeping it real with you since the day yo' mother pushed you outta her womb."

"True, true," Tiaz nodded. His old man was right. He always kept it one-hundred stacks with him.

Melvin placed the black book back inside of the safe and shut it. He then motioned for his son to sit down on the bed and he sat down beside him.

"Truthfully, I should have been stopped doing this shit. I was only doing it to be able to pay the rent up for a few months and get the bills from outta my hair," he spoke honestly. "I got that money and then some."

"Then why did you keep on going?"

"When I lost your mother I felt dead inside. I was a walking, talking zombie. I was alive, but I wasn't exactly living. It wasn't until I picked up that mask and that gun that I felt alive again, son. The rush and high I got outta making those fools out there part with their money and drugs," he looked ahead at nothing as he clenched his fists tightly, causing veins to bulge in his hands. From the look on his father's face Tiaz could tell that he was passionate about what he was talking about. "Man, I tell you. It made me an adrenaline junkie. The action, the drama, the threat of knowing that shit could go down bad at any given time put me on cloud nine. I couldn't get enough, so I kept doing it and doing it," the excitement left his eyes and he rested his hands on his knees. "I was all in with this shit until I got the scare of my life."

"Oh, yeah? What was that, pop?" Tiaz' forehead wrinkled with concern.

"Tonight, when you took those bullets that was meant for me. I thought I had lost you forever," Melvin placed his hand on Tiaz' shoulder. At that moment, for the first time, Tiaz saw the glassiness in his father's eyes and knew that he was on the verge of shedding tears. This was as vulnerable as he had ever seen him. He was so used to him being solemn and without much emotion. "I lost my queen, I'm not tryna lose my prince. The more I think about it. I had no business bringing you in on this thing of mine. It was far too dangerous. I'm sure your mother is turning over in her grave right now."

Staring into his father's eyes, Tiaz could definitely feel his hurt. He loved his father immensely and he didn't want to see him crying. He really didn't want to stop getting it how he lived either, but if it was going to make his old man feel better, then he was going to turn his back on the game.

Tiaz rose from off his seat and paced the floor with his hands on his hips, thinking. He licked his lips and massaged his chin. Suddenly, he stopped and looked to his father.

"Alright, pop, I'll give this up, but only on one condition. We gotta get out in the field one more time. I'm asking that we hit one last lick, just one," he held up his finger and looked at his old man with serious eyes.

Melvin ran his hand down his face and took a deep breath. He looked up at his son and said, "Why?"

"Why what, pop?"

"Why do you need to do this last job? We gotta 'nough paypa to blow town right this minute. We wouldn't even need to pack. We could just go, just hop into my car and drive."

"Well, I'ma tell you the truth, straight up. It's like you use to tell me, you don't bullshit a bullshitter."

"That's right."

"There this nigga named Cordell; he's got the streets on smash with his work. He's arrogant, flamboyant, runs his mouth and thinks he's God. The mothafucka believes that there ain't nobody out here with balls big enough to rob his ass."

"Lemme guess, you gotta show 'em you that nigga with balls, right?"

"You right, pop. I gots to be that nigga," Tiaz smiled and placed his hand on his father's shoulder, looking into his eyes.

"You know, if you swat a beehive enough times you'll eventually get stung, right?"

"I hear you, OG. But I gotta show this fool that my daddy didn't raise no mark. 'Fore as long as I got guns and heart, I'ma bring it to any nigga, you feeling me?"

"Yep," he nodded and interlocked his fingers underneath his chin. Staring ahead, he thought long and hard about what his son was asking him to do. He knew all about Cordell, and he wasn't anything to play with from what he heard. He knew that there would be consequences and repercussions if the crack king found out that him and his son robbed him. Still, he was contemplating on riding with his son on this last lick. Although he wanted to, he couldn't back out. Not now. Growing up, his son had always looked up to him like he was something special. Although Melvin knew otherwise, he didn't want to taint that image that his offspring had of him.

"Fuck it! We gone roll. One more job isn't gone hurt us. We'll get in and get out," Melvin said as he rose to his feet and outstretched his hand to his son. "Put her there, partner," he said, refered to him shaking his hand.

Upon hearing his father's answer, Tiaz broke out in a wide smile and hugged him. This caused his father to smile and he embraced him. They then broke their hug and stepped back from one another.

"Like I was saying," Melvin began, "we gone roll out on this one. But as soon as we pull this caper, we getting the fuck outta dodge, deal?"

"Deal," Tiaz dapped up his old man and sealed the deal. Melvin then kissed him on the side of his head and patted him on his back affectionately. Although it wasn't the 'I love you, son' Tiaz was looking for it still made him feel good.

\*\*\*

Tiaz and Melvin walked around the living room dousing everything with gasoline. Once Melvin was done, he tossed his gas can aside causing it to spill some of its contents. Still holding on to his gas can, Tiaz stood over the trap niggaz. He watched as they squeezed their eyelids shut and shook their heads, blowing their noses as the overwhelming odor of gasoline burned their nostrils. The men gagged and huffed feeling the fumes of the flammable liquid invading their lungs, threatening to poison them. Fearful of losing their lives, they squirmed around trying to get free.

"I ain't gone kill you niggaz, man. Nah, this shit here is bigger than you and me. See, this shit is about an old nigga that thinks the G shit he laid down in the eighties still holds up today. This my way of telling 'em, nah, you may have pumped fear into niggaz back in the day. But chu definitely ain't pumping fear into this mothafucka standing right here!" Tiaz smacked his hand up against his bulletproof vest which was strapped over his upper body. With that said, he approached the coffee table where wrinkled stacks of money, a block and a half of cocaine, and four black handguns resided. He poured what was left of the gasoline on the items on the coffee table before tossing the gas can aside. He then watched as his father drew a machete and went down the row of trap niggaz slicing off their gags and bondages.

Melvin then opened the door to the crack house and stood aside, allowing the terrified men to escape. The men stood where they were. They were afraid that it was a trick and they were going to get slaughtered if they moved.

"Y'all niggaz gotta choice," Tiaz began, striking a bluish yellow flame with his Zippo lighter. "You can either haul ass outta the door, or stay here and perish with Cordell's house and all the rest of his shit." Having stated that, Tiaz dropped the Zippo lighter onto the items on the coffee table and everything went up in flames, instantly. Seeing the fire sweep all around the living room, the trap niggaz ran out of the burning house. Crossing the threshold out of the yard, they all scattered in different directions screaming and hollering.

Melvin sheathed his machete and made his way out of the door. Tiaz gave the house one last look, watching as the flames ripped throughout the living room. Satisfied, he strolled out of the door. He came down the steps and found his father sitting behind the wheel of the getaway car.

Tiaz was halfway out of the yard when the house exploded with a golden orange light. Fire erupted out of the windows, sending flames and broken glass rushing out into the night's air. The young nigga didn't even flinch; he kept right along walking until he'd cleared the yard. Once he was in the passenger seat of the vehicle, his father threw the gear into *drive* and pulled off.

The message that Tiaz left was clear. He definitely had balls big enough to oppose Cordell.

Tranay Adams

## CHAPTER EIGHTEEN

Melvin pulled into the back parking lot of The Bar Fly and killed the engine. He then looked to Tiaz who was staring out of the window.

"You good, son?" Melvin asked Tiaz of his injuries from being shot.

"I'm okay, pop."

"Alright then, you got that nigga J-Murda's chain?"

"Is a fish's pussy waterproof?" He held up a black velvet bag with golden drawstrings.

Melvin smiled and said, "Cool. This a bar and you not 'pose to be in here 'less you at least twenty-one. You look older than your age though, so just in case anyone asks, you twenty-two. They ask for identification, then you reach for your wallet, and suddenly remember you forgot it back home. Got it?"

"Got it."

"Okay then," Melvin pulled out his gun and checked its magazine. He then smacked it back into the butt of his weapon and cocked the slide on it. The sound of clinging metal ripped through the interior of the vehicle. "Let's roll."

Tiaz and his old man hopped out of the car and made their way towards the entrance of The Bar Fly.

"Yo, pop, I gotta take a leak."

"When we get in here, gone and handle yo' business," he told him. "I'm sure I can hold it down. I don't expect shit outta this meeting, there will be too many witnesses in here for a nigga to try some dumb shit."

As soon as Melvin and Tiaz pushed open the heavy wooden door of The Bar Fly they were enveloped by the dimly lit establishment. They stood where they were taking in the bar. There were people sitting around swigging cold ones and shooting the breeze, dancing around to the music pumping from the juke-box against the wall or playing pool.

Melvin spotted Chief at a pool table playing a game against a stocky cat wearing an apple jack and a bushy mustache. The man took the occasional swig of his Miller Lite as he watched Chief handle his business on the table.

"It's clean up time, Jerry," Chief announced to the nigga he was playing a game of pool with. His eyes looked to the bar and found Melvin. He gave him a nod of acknowledgement and he returned it. Jerry then focused on the ball he was trying to drop into one of the pockets of the pool table.

"Clean up time? Nigga, you stay talking shit, just shoot the gotdamn ball, man." Jerry said annoyed. Chief was kicking his black ass on the pool table and making him look bad in the eyes of his woman. Now, he was feeling humiliated because he'd been bragging to her all night how he was the grandmaster of shooting pool and no one could fuck with him. "Whatever, homeboy, you just have my paypa once I'm done handing you your ass in this here game." Chief said and stuck his tongue out of the side of his mouth. He zoomed in on the shot he had in mind, teases the ball with being hit by his pool stick. Abruptly, the stick struck the ball and it went flying towards the pocket he had in mind. He took the shot and the ball he planned on hitting dropped into its intended pocket.

After taking the shot, Chief stood up straight talking shit and sharpening his stick with the blue cube. Looking to the bar, Chief signaled for Melvin to give him a second and took a sip from a glass of brown liquor. He then sat the glass down and leaned over the pool table, focusing on wrapping up the game.

"The bathroom is down that hall and to your left," Melvin pointed, directing Tiaz the men's room. "I'ma cop a squat at this bar and order myself a lil taste."

"Okay, pop." Tiaz handed his old man the velvet bag and went to relieve his bladder.

Melvin sat down at the bar and motioned the bartender over, ordering up a Hennessy over the rocks. Once he'd gotten his drink, he slowly sipped it and glanced back over his shoulder at Chief. He found him winking and smiling at Jerry's lady, boasting his gold crown tooth. She returned the gesture and Jerry gave her the evil eye. Chief then turned his attention back to the game at hand.

"Man, I had to piss like a race horse." Tiaz said, returning from the rest room. He took up the stool beside Melvin and grabbed a handful of cashews from out of the bowl on bar top, tossing them back. "So, is he here yet, OG?"

"Yeah, he's here. He's playing a pool game," he responded, keeping his eyes on Chief at the pool table.

"Which one is he?" Tiaz asked, having turned around on his stool.

"Right there," Melvin nodded to Chief. "He's the one that's about to take the next shot, at the center table there."

"Got cha," Tiaz shook the cashews in his fist before tossing them back into his mouth, munching them.

"Pop, there's something I been meaning to ask you."

"Spit it out, son," Melvin took another sip of his drink.

"Since, uh, you know, popped your cherry with that the other night...how do you feel?" He asked him of his first time killing in cold blood the night he hit Shivs's people's house. Although he was a street nigga he'd never murdered anyone before, and he never thought he'd have to either. But that changed once he chose the ski mask way.

Melvin took a sip of his drink and hissed as he felt the liquid fire pouring down his throat. He licked his lips and swirled the dark liquor around in his glass.

"Let's just say it takes a really cold, calloused, sick and twisted mothafucka to murder someone in cold blood and not feel any kind of remorse afterwards. It's easy to aim a gun at someone. It's not easy to actually pull the trigger, 'cause when you take another man's life, you gotta live with that for the rest of yours. You're the one that's gonna see that man's face you murdered every time you shut your eyes." As Melvin spoke his mind he was assaulted with excessive flashbacks of the night he murdered Shivs, Tamara, and her man. There were muzzle flashes, blood, and horrified screams. Everything seemed to have happened inside his head theatrically. "So, before a man ever pulls a gun to take a life, he's gotta ask himself. Am I ready to live the rest of my life with the memories of this man's death haunting me and never going away?"

Tiaz frowned. If what his father was saying was true then he was the cold, calloused, sick, twisted mothafucka that he was referring to. He had never been haunted by the lives he'd taken. In fact, Tiaz never felt anything about anyone that had fallen victim to his gun. The way he saw it, they were in his way of progress and they had to be eliminated.

"You mean, the people you killed haunt chu?" Tiaz inquired.

"Hell yeah, they haunt me," Melvin said, turning around on his stool and sitting his glass down on the bar top. He then reached inside of his overcoat and pulled out a pack of Newport 100s. "There are a couple of them in here with us right now," Tiaz looked around the bar with a confused expression on his face. He didn't see any dead people that may be around them. "Don't bother. You can't see 'em, son, but they're here. They all have the same holes from the bullets I put in 'em, too."

"Really?"

Melvin lit up one of the Newports and blew out smoke. He nodded and said, "Yep."

"Well, are they saying anything?"

"Mostly bitching about how I was wrong for peeling their caps back, and how they didn't deserve to die. They piss and moan from time to time," Melvin tapped the cigarette and dumped ashes into a clear glass ashtray that the bartender had just sat before him. "I'll tell you this. I didn't give it to anybody that didn't have it coming. They were all scumbags and pieces of shit, just like me. One day it will be my turn, and when The Grim Reaper comes knocking, I'll open the door and embrace my fate like the man that I am."

"Respect," Tiaz nodded, admiring his old man acceptance of his fate whenever Judgment Day came.

"Gotdamn it!"

A shrill came from Tiaz and Melvin's rear. They looked over their shoulders just in time to see the man Chief had been shooting pool with, Jerry, throw his pool stick to the floor.

Jerry reached into the pocket of his slacks and pulled out a gold money clip. After peeling off a few crisp bills, he tossed them on the pool table and snagged his woman's arm on his way out of the door. The woman stumbled forward nearly falling from him pulling her along so fast. Jerry crossed Tiaz and Melvin's path, cursing up a storm under his breath.

Chief threw on his suit's jacket and buttoned it up. Smiling, he snatched up his winnings, folded them up and shoved them inside of his pocket. Chief then made his way in Tiaz and Melvin's direction. Whilst in motion, he glanced at the Rolex on his wrist. Finally reaching the man he had made arrangements with to meet, he sat down on the stool beside him.

"Scotch, Nigel," Chief threw his finger up at the bartender.

Nigel nodded and began making Chief's drink.

"You got something that's gonna make me smile?" Chief asked Melvin.

Melvin nodded and said, "Yep, and its right here." He looked around cautiously before passing him the black velvet bag with the gold drawstrings.

Chief thanked Nigel when he brought his drink back and sat it on top of a napkin. He then opened the velvet bag and peered inside. A smile broadened his face once he saw J- Murda's blood speckled gold chain.

Chief closed the bag back up and sat it aside on the bar top. He interlocked his hands and leaned closer to Melvin, so everyone wouldn't be able to hear what they were discussing.

"Did this cock sucker die screaming?"

"Like a fourth grade sissy."

"Oh, really?"

"Yep, cashed 'em out," Melvin told him. "He'll definitely have a closed casket funeral."

"Good," Chief took a sip of his drink. He then pulled a thick manila envelope from inside of his suit and placed it on the empty stool beside him. Discreetly, Melvin picked the envelope up and tucked it inside of his overcoat.

"Keep in mind the last thing we discussed regarding my wife. Although the verdict isn't in on that yet, when it is…" Chief didn't finish what he had to say, he just gave him a knowing look. Melvin picked right up on it, too.

"I got cha. Beena pleasure," Melvin shook his hand. He then swallowed the last of his drink and rose to his feet. Melvin patted Chief on the back then said goodbye to him. He motioned for Tiaz to follow him as he made a beeline towards the door.

***

A black on black Mercedes Benz pulled up across the street from the Western Inn motel in The City of Lawndale. Its passenger side door opened and Cordell stepped out, one Air Force One at a time. His five foot ten stature filled out a black Nike track suit, which he wore zipped up to his chin. He wore a trench coat over his track suit. He also had a Nike bucket hat pulled down low over his brows.

Once Cordell was out of the car and in full view, he took a good look around to make sure that he wasn't being watched. When he was convinced that there wasn't anyone watching him, he ducked back inside of the vehicle and pulled out a silver .357. After he checked the chamber of the weapon to make sure that it was fully loaded, he snapped it back closed. He then took in his surroundings before lifting the bottom of his jacket's suit and stashing his revolver inside of his waistline.

"Keep the car runnin', I'll be back in a second," Cordell told Sharayne. He went to slam the door shut but stopped once she called for his attention. "'Sup?"

"Gimme a kiss, babe," Sharayne told him, blowing a pink bubble with the gum she was chewing.

"Hmmm, have you been a good bitch?" He angled his head and grinned.

"Oh yes, I've been a very, very, very good bitch." She smiled proudly.

"Well, alright. I guess you earned it," he leaned back inside of the Benz and tongued her down, while rubbing the side of her neck. Pulling away, he kissed her twice more on the lips and pulled out of the Mercedes. Having slammed the door shut behind him, he looked both ways before jogging across the street. Staring through the large window of the motel, Sharayne watched Cordell approach the clerk and place something on the desk top that she believed was money. The clerk, who was laid back in his chair with his feet propped up watching TV, sat up quickly. He snatched a pair of keys from off the hook of a wall filled with hanging motel keys. He tossed the keys up in the air towards Cordell and he snatched them out of the air. He then gave the clerk a nod and made his way out of the establishment. The last thing that Sharayne saw before turning on the stereo to listen to music was, the clerk holding up the one hundred dollar bill Cordell had given him to examine it for authenticity. Seeing that the bill was indeed real, he folded it up and slid it inside of his pocket. Afterwards, he nestled his hands in his lap and continued watching the television.

\*\*\*

Cordell looked for the room door that matched the number on the key that the desk clerk had given him. He didn't find it until he was on the second tier at the center door. He unlocked the door and found the man he was looking for. Home was at the center of two naked, busty white women. They both had their head lying against his bare chest and were fast asleep. Cordell shut the door behind him quietly and turned on the lamp's light that was sitting on the nightstand beside the bed. As soon as the light came on the man he'd came to pay a visit upon face winced, and he smacked his lips as if he tasted something flavorful.

Cordell looked to the nightstand to find a cellular phone, the room key that's identical to the one in his possession, and a handgun. Cordell picked up the weapon and checked its magazine. Seeing that it was fully loaded, he smacked it back into the bottom of the gun. He then pointed it at homeboy lying in the bed between the two women. He held the gun on him as if he was thinking about shooting him in the face, but he was really thinking about how easy it would have been to kill him off. Shaking his head and thinking about how his enforcer was slipping, he then picked up the man's cell phone. Seeing that he had *16 missed calls*, all he was sure belonged to him seeing as how that's how many times he'd contacted him. Cordell shook his head again and sat the device back down where he'd picked it up from.

Placing his fist to his mouth, Cordell cleared his throat and hid the gun he'd picked up off the nightstand behind his back. He then shut his eyelids briefly and took a deep breath. Disguising his voice to sound like someone else, he spat loud and clear, "Where the mothafucking money at, nigga?"

"Huh?" The groggily and disoriented man's eyelids popped open and he went to grab his handgun from off the nightstand. His heart dropped when he didn't find his banga there. Whoever had snuck into his motel room had him dead to rights, and he just knew that he was a dead man.

"Looking for this, mothafucka?" Cordell spat with his disguised voice and pointed the man's own gun at him, pulling the trigger. The banga clicked empty and the man nearly leaped out of his skin, his heart thudding madly. He had been expecting the gun to send him to eternal damnation. Cordell lowered the gun and flipped on the light switch, exposing his true identity.

"I coulda knocked your noodles loose from your head and them two Lily white bitches, too. You slipping, youngsta, you slipping bad."

By this time, the white girls slowly came awake, blinking their eyelids and wiping them. When they looked up and saw Cordell with the gun in his hand they were instantly shook. Terror was inside of their eyes and their hearts were beating fast.

"What's going on here, Savino?" One of the white girls asked.

"Beat it, bitches!" Cordell spoke with authority. Instantly, the girls hopped out of bed and slipped on their dresses. Grabbing their high heel pumps, they headed for the door which Cordell held open for them. Once they'd crossed the threshold over onto the tier, he shut the door quietly and pulled out his own gun. He sat at the foot of the bed watching as Savino pulled on his boxer briefs and his Dickies. His gold crucifix moved from left to right as he looped it around his neck. "I can't believe this shit, you out here knee deep into some pussy while one of my crack houses were getting hit. On top of that, I'm calling and calling your fucking phone and you're not answering the mothafucka."

"My bad, boss dawg, a nigga stay on the money; I hadn't been up in no pussy in a minute. I was just tryna get straight. You feel me?" He slipped his wife beater over his head and began tucking it inside of his jeans.

Cordell took a deep breath and ran his hand down his face. He then looked over at Savino. "You know what? I'll admit, you have been on yo' shit, and I haven't given you any down time in a while. A man has needs; I know that, so I'ma let this shit slide. But from now on, you keep that cellular glued to you and off of silent. You got that?"

Savino slipped his sweatshirt on over his head and straightened it out. Afterwards, he pulled his gold necklace from out of his collar and laid it down on his chest, so that his platinum Jesus piece would be visible. "Yeah," he nodded his understanding. "I got that."

"Good. Now get out there and find the mothafuckaz that hit my shit," Cordell extended Savino's gun to him. He took it and tucked it at the small of his back. He then threw on his leather jacket and pulled on his Raiders beanie. Next, he opened the door for Cordell to exit and followed out right behind him.

The streets would run with blood if he didn't get his hands on the mothafuckaz that hit his boss's crack house.

## CHAPTER NINETEEN

Melvin pulled up across the street from Threat's house and killed the engine of his vehicle. Tiaz hopped out of the car and jogged across the street, looking both ways as he went along. He made his way up the driveway and by passed the front door of his homeboy's house. It was eleven o'clock at night. He didn't want to knock on the front door and wake up Threat's grandmother, so he opted to go to the backyard and knock on his bedroom's window instead.

Making it to the backyard, Tiaz was surprised to find Threat standing up on the back porch smoking a bleezy. The light was out, and all he could make out was the shape of his homeboy and the ember end of the blunt he was smoking. It was from the repugnant odor of the weed that Tiaz knew that his brother from another had some fire on his hands. Threat took the blunt from out of his mouth with his left hand and abruptly whipped around, drawing his .45 from out of his waistline. He pointed the gun at Tiaz and stopped him dead in his tracks. Having frozen where he was, Tiaz slowly lifted his hands up into the air, palms showing.

"Who that?" Threat asked in a hushed and menacing tone.

"It's me, homeboy…Tiaz."

"Oh," the hostility drained from Threat's voice and he returned his banga from where he'd drawn it. "What chu doing creeping around here this late?" He slapped hands with Tiaz and embraced him with a gangsta hug.

"I just wanted to bring you a couple of thangs, comrade," he told him.

"Oh, yeah? What's that?"

Tiaz lifted up his hoodie and revealed stacks of money lining his waist. He pulled out every stack and stacked them on top of one another on the windowpane.

"That's you, right there, loved one," Tiaz pointed to the stacks of money.

"For real? That's love, homie." Threat slapped hands with his homeboy and embraced him.

"That's not all..." Tiaz took off J-Murda's chain and looped it around Threat's neck. Threat in turn picked up the gold and diamond logo from off his chest, looking at it. His brows furrowed because he didn't know who J-Murda was. "I know what chu thinking. J-Murda's one of the fools that helped pack us out in that alley that night."

"You took 'em out, Crim?"

"Yep. Don't nobody fuck with us, my nigga. 'Cause if they do they getting it off top. I don't give a fuck who they are. Bloods, crips, eses, Asians, mafias, cartels...whoever come at us, I'ma put blood in they mouth, straight like that."

"That's love."

"Fa sho'."

"Man, you out here doing licks that's netting you paypa like that," he looked to the money stacked on the windowpane. "And you ain't put cha man on?"

"Man, pop, ain't tryna..."

"Pop's?" Threat tilted his head down and looked at him like he couldn't be serious, "You hitting licks with cho old man?"

"Yeah," Tiaz answered. He didn't mean to tell him that he and his father where doing dirt together. It just slipped. It wasn't that he didn't trust his main man with the knowledge; it was just that he wanted to keep his hand close to his chest. "He only agreed to let me get down if I kept it between us. That's why I can't put chu down with us. Otherwise, you know you'd be right there with me. You know how we do." He outstretched his hand.

"Straight up," Threat slapped hands with his crime partner and embraced him.

"Lemme get outta here, man, pop's parked out front waiting on a nigga."

"Alright, be safe, my nigga."

"All the time."

Threat looked on at his homeboy until he'd disappeared from out of the backyard. He then looked down at the chain around his neck. At that moment, he knew that he'd be down for Tiaz forever. He'd ride or die for that young nigga. He'd starved with him and he'd eaten with him. They were as thick as thieves. And although Tiaz was only fifteen years old, he was the realest nigga he knew and he loved him to death.

\*\*\*

Crackhead Jerome sat chained to an iron chair with his head bowed. He was wearing a white T-shirt that was stained pink around the collar from his bleeding and tattered jeans. His bare, dirty feet were planted firmly on the floor, and splashes of his blood were over the floor as well as on his foot. He was sitting on a spot light provided by the illuminating yellowish bulb that dangled from the ceiling. A couple of flies swarmed around the dull bulb as it flickered on and off, threatening to turn out completely.

The basement that he was inside of was void of any furniture. It was clean from wall to wall and from ceiling to floor. The only thing that could be heard inside of the dimly lit space was the dripping of a leaking pipe in the ceiling that created several growing puddles of water on the floor.

A shadow approached Jerome and put him in shade. His head bobbed about as he looked up at the man that had been beating him for the past two and a half hours. Both of his eyes were nearly swollen shut and his lips were twice their size. His nose was broken and bleeding. His nose was also crooked on his face from being punched so many times. The crackhead's face and neck were slicked wet from perspiration and blood. Despite his appearance, the man that had abducted him didn't show him any mercy. He wanted the whereabouts of the men that had robbed his boss's crack house, and he wasn't going to stop punishing him until he forfeited information that could led to their capture.

Jerome stared up at the nigga that had kidnapped him. He watched as he took a bottle of Hennessy to the head and turned the bottle up. His throat rolled up and down his neck as he guzzled the alcohol beverage. He was in a blood speckled wife beater and Dickie's. His hands were fitted in a pair of black leather gloves and a .9mm automatic handgun was stashed at the front of his pants.

"This that Hen Doggy Dog, boy! Whooo!" Savino said like a drunken fraternity brother as he looked at the bottle of Hennessy in his hand. He then turned his eyes on Jerome. "You want some, my nigga? Here, you can have the bottle homie." He slammed the Hennessy bottle against the side of Jerome's head and it exploded. Upon impact, dark liquor and broken glass went flying everywhere. The brute force of the blow left Jerome bleeding from the side of his head. He threw his head back, squeezing his eyelids shut and gritting his teeth in agony. He tried to fight back the pain, but it was overwhelming to him.

"Ahhh, fuck, man, fuck!" Jerome complained in excruciation. "I keep telling you, I don't know nothing, man. Why can't chu believe me, huh? Why can't chu trust what I tell you is the truth?" He hissed like a snake as he encountered a throbbing migraine.

Savino kneeled down to Jerome and looked him square in his eyes. He wore a dead serious expression as he went onto speak, "Youz a mothafucking crackhead, yo' word don't mean jack shit. I know you know something, you got to. You be all up through this hood selling shit, stealing shit, and mingling with niggaz. You cling to the shadows and watch the happenings in the streets from afar. So I know you either saw something or heard something about the mothafuckaz that hit my boss man's spot. Come on now, think on it. There's gotta be something."

"Okay, alright," Jerome swallowed the lump of fear that was in his throat. He squeezed his eyelids shut and clenched his jaws as he thought on it. "Think, think, think, think," he told himself, still squeezing his eyelids shut. When he couldn't think of any information to tell Savino, he peeled his eyelids back open to speak. "I'm sorry, man, but I don't know nothing."

Disappointment came across Savino's face and he stood back up, pulling his .9mm automatic from off his waistline. He pointed it at either of Jerome's kneecaps and pulled the trigger. Blood splat out of the gunshot wounds that had been put in Jerome's knees and smoke rose from out of them. A mad dogging Savino stood tall and glared down at Jerome's miserable ass. His chest rose and fell as he breathed huskily, holding his smoking gun in his gloved hand.

"Aaaahhhhh! My knees, my fucking knees!" Jerome complained of all of the pain he was experiencing having been shot through the knees. "You bastard! You miserable fucking bastard."

"Now, I'm gonna ask you one more time before I gone 'head and put an end to this shit. Who are these fools that jacked Cordell's spot? Take yo' time and think carefully now, 'cause yo' life depends on it."

Jerome gritted his teeth harder and harder. His eyebrows arched and his nose scrunched up. He was trying his best to combat the fire in his kneecaps, but the agony was too great for him.

"Alright, I got…I got something," Jerome told him.

Savino smiled and said, "That a boy, I knew you wouldn't let me down. Now spit it out."

"Okay. There's this nigga that I sold a couple of bulletproof vests to a minute ago. He had already bought one, but he caught up with me to buy another one," he winced and gritted his teeth because his knees were killing him.

"Yeah, so, what's the big deal 'bout the nigga buying a bulletproof vest? Get to the meat of the story."

"When I sold him the last vest he had this young nigga with him. He couldn't be any older than fifteen or sixteen years old. He was big as hell, too, you could tell that lil' mothafucka lifted weights. He was built like a goddamn superhero," Jerome winced some more and threw his head back, squirming in his seat from all of his aching and suffering. "Anyway, while I was there, I overheard the boy say that the hood better watch out for them, 'cause they were going to take shit over as jack boys. Lil' homie said anybody could get robbed, and he didn't give a fuck about who it was."

"I have to admit, you have garnered my interest." Savino admitted as he massaged his chin. "I'm willing to bet dollas to donuts that those are the two that hit my man's spot. You get any names?"

"Yeah, gemme a minute, though," Jerome bowed his head and thought on it for a minute. He then looked back up at Savino. "Okay, alright, I remember. I think their names are…Melvin and Tiaz. Yeah, that's it, Melvin and Tiaz."

As soon as he said Tiaz, Savino's eyelids stretched wide open in shock. He then scowled and clenched his jaws, asking, "You gotta be shitting me?"

"Naw, man, this is the honest to God truth. You gotta believe me, man! You gotta believe me!" He whimpered and tears dripped from his eyes. He was petrified of dying and he seriously hoped that Savino was going to spare his life.

"Oh, I believe you," Savino told him. "Hold this for me," he sat his 9 Double M on Jerome's lap and reached into his back pocket to pull out a small black book and an ink pen. He opened the book and placed the pen to the first blank line. He went on to jot down all of the information that he'd been relayed. "Now, you gotta address for me?"

"Yeah, I got one. I went over there to drop off the vest presonally..." Jerome went on to tell Savino the address where he could find Tiaz and his father. Once Savino had finished writing everything down, he placed the small book and the ink pen into his back pocket.

"Thanks, man, you were a big help," Savino picked the .9mm automatic handgun up from Jerome's lap and stood up straight. He then pointed the deadly end of his weapon at the crackhead's forehead.

Jerome's eyes bulged and he gasped. He went to say something, but by then, his blood and brain fragments went flying out the back of his nappy head.

*** 

A man walked down the sidewalk leading a dog along on a leash and looking for a place for it to shit. He was just about to cross paths with the old abandoned house that was boarded up.

*Bloc!*

Light flashed from the window of the basement as Savino continued to open fire. The sudden burst of gunfire startled the man walking his dog and he hurried away in the opposite direction.

*Bloc! Bloc!*

***

Savino lowered his smoking weapon and looked at his handiwork. He then dropped the gun to the floor and pulled the leather glove from off his right hand with his teeth. Taking the glove, he stuffed it into his back pocket and pulled out his cellular phone. He speed dialed Cordell and placed the phone to his ear.

"Boss dawg, I got something that's gonna put me back in your good graces..." Savino smiled.

***

Dawn was approaching so the sky was navy blue, with the sun slowly rising. The streets were scarce with cars. Occasionally, one would fly past, making that sound that automobiles make when they are driven fast. The last vehicle to come past was a '92 Ford Taurus, crossing a red stop light like it was good to go. The stop light turned green and a '72 Chevy F-150 pickup drove out into the intersection, stopping at a stop sign. The old heap was a rusty brown with mix match doors, looking like it had seen better days. It wasn't much to look at but it got its owner where he needed to be. The driver threw the raggedy Chevy in *park*. The truck's engine made a continuous loud noise, like a vehicle of its time, smoke wafting out of its exhaust pipes. The back red lights of the F-150 as well as its bubble headlights were the only lights seen in the dim lighting of the day. The front passenger door of the truck opened and a man wearing a bandana over the lower half of his face hopped out with a potato sack. He removed a step stool from the flat bed and looked both ways, making sure there wasn't anyone around to witness what he was about to do. Having made sure that the coast was clear, the man set the step stool before the stop sign and walked up to the top of it. Opening the potato sack, the man pulled out Crackhead

Jerome's mutilated severed head. He stuffed the sack into his back pocket and held the severed head in both hands, studying its face. "Poor bastard," the man placed the head on top of the stop sign's pole. After pulling it down, he made sure that it would stay in place. Having seen that it was secure, he stepped down from the step stool and picked it up. He hurried over to the truck and tossed it into the flat bed. Jumping back inside of the pickup, he slammed the door shut and motioned for the driver to pull off.

\*\*\*

*An hour later*

People crowded the street like there was a parade going on, all of them staring up at the head planted on top of the stop sign's pole. Some of them were in shock while the others wondered who'd put it there and for what reason. The street niggaz that were in the audience knew exactly who the head belonged to and who had ordered it to be put there. They received Cordell's message. *Anyone that was against him would meet their demise.* This was for all the mothafuckaz that may have thought that he'd gotten soft. This message would give them a rude awakening.

## CHAPTER TWENTY
### *That night*

"Alright, you got everything, son?" Melvin asked Tiaz. They were standing inside of the living room with their luggage in their hands.

Tiaz looked around the living room and thought on it for a moment. There wasn't anything that he'd forgotten.

"Yeah, pop. That's everything."

"Alright then, let's get up on outta here," Melvin made his way towards the front door with Tiaz bringing up the rear. Reaching the front door, he stopped in his tracks and narrowed his eyelids. The expression he had on his face was of a man that had something on his mind. "Shit," he turned around to his son.

"'Sup, pop?" Tiaz' forehead wrinkled.

"Here I was asking you if you forgot anything, and I'm the one leaving something behind," he shook his head shamefully and sat his luggage down, addressing his son. "Stay right here, I'll be right back."

Melvin journeyed back into his bedroom and flipped on the light switch. Standing in the doorway, he looked around the bedroom with furrowed brows, looking for something that was very sentimental to him.

A smile broadened Melvin's face when he saw the portrait that he'd left behind lying on the bed. He approached the portrait and picked it up, looking over it. Inside the frame was a photograph of him kissing his pregnant wife on her protruding belly. The smile that was already on his face grew that much broader seeing the joy that was on him and his wife's face. Kissing the portrait, he slid it inside of his overcoat. He then made his way to the door and stepped on top of something on the floor. Once he went to take another step, he tripped over it and fell on his back. Lying where he was on the floor, he stared up at the ceiling, chest rising and falling easily.

Melvin looked up from where he was on the floor and saw what he'd tripped over. It was a grenade. In addition to the guns, ammo and silencers that he'd bought from Gatz, he copped a few grenades from him as well. At the time he didn't know what the hell he'd need some grenades for, but he figured that it was better to be safe than sorry, so he copped about eight of them.

Getting back upon his feet, Melvin walked over to the grenade and picked it up. He shoved it inside of his overcoat's pocket and advanced towards the door, flipping off the light switch on his way out. He shut the door behind him and made his way down the hallway. The closer he got to the living room he noticed that Tiaz wasn't standing at the door like he was before he'd left him to get the portrait. Instead, he saw both of their luggages at the door. Melvin's forehead creased and he looked from left to right as he drew closer to the living room. It wasn't until he crossed the threshold into the living room that he saw what was going on.

Melvin found Tiaz sitting in a chair at the center of the floor. Savino stood behind him with his .9mm automatic handgun pointed to the back of his dome. The young nigga'z neck was stiff and his eyes were staring out of their corners, trying to see exactly what it was Savino was doing. He knew that if he was to so much as flinch homeboy would send his brain flying from out of his forehead.

Besides Savino, there were three other men in the living room. Two of them were dressed in all black and wore black sunglasses and black bandanas over the lower half of their faces. Down at their sides, they gripped AK-47s with both hands. These men were posted up on either side of the front door, both mad dogging Melvin.

The third man was sitting on the couch with a silver .357 Magnum revolver lying in his lap which he held firmly. He was in a porkpie hat and linen suit, which he wore underneath his overcoat.

"Melvin, right?" Cordell asked. He took the time to pull a Black & Mild out of his overcoat and stuck it into his mouth.

"Yeah, that's me," Melvin confirmed, keeping his eyes on Tiaz. He saw the danger that his son was in and it made him uneasy. If it wasn't for the fact that he and Tiaz had stashed their guns in the hidden compartments inside of their car, he would have drawn heat and set it off in that bitch. "Is all of that necessary?" He nodded to Savino who still had his gun pointed to the back of Tiaz' dome.

"I'm afraid so, you'll have to excuse me if I don't have mercy. But that lil' cock sucka of yours stole from me." Cordell patted himself down for a lighter. When he discovered one, he pulled it out and tried to light up his thin cigar. A flame wouldn't form so one of his men stepped forth and lit his Black & Mild with his own lighter. Cordell, then, waved him back and puffed on his Black. Tilting his head back, he blew out a roar of smoke and focused his attention back on Melvin. "You see, Melvin, I detest thieves. To me, they're the lowest form. They're right up there with rapists, snitches and child molesters."

"You can stop this shit now! I already know what this is about! You came here for some get-back 'cause me and my boy hit that spot of yours. Yeah, mothafucka, we hit it and what?" Melvin spat angrily. His eyebrows sloped and his nose scrunched up. His jaws were clenched so tight that his bone structure showed. "What the fuck are you gone do about it?"

"That's right, pop! Fuck these mothafuckaz!" Tiaz roared with spit flying from off his lips. "Show 'em how we cut, we ain't scared of shit! We Petties, Petties, mothafuckaz! Petties!" He looked around at all of the men that posed threats to him and his father.

"Shut the fuck up, lil' nigga!" Savino smacked Tiaz upside the back of his dome with the butt of his gun. The young nigga winced as his head lurched forward. Burgundy blood ran from the back of his head and slid down his neck.

"Say something else, and I swear before God and heaven I'ma put that ass on mute forever!" Savino threatened, murder dancing in his pupils. His trigger finger was itching and if Tiaz disobeyed him then he was going to blow his head off.

"Put cho goddamn hands on my son again and see what happens!" Melvin hollered out to Savino, pointing his finger at him as he held onto something inside of his overcoat's pocket.

"Fuck you gone do, nigga? We got the drop on yo' monkey ass!" Savino shot back.

"Like I said, 'touch my boy again' and see what happens!" He threatened with his nostrils flaring and his jaws pulsating.

"What chu gone do, pussy?" Savino challenged.

"This what the fuck I'm gone do, nigga!" Melvin pulled the grenade from out of his pocket and pulled the pin. He kept a firm grip on its trigger though, so it wouldn't explode in his hand. He then held the grenade above his head and looked around the room at all of his enemies. All of them niggaz were looking shook except Cordell. As soon as he whipped the grenade out their asses panicked and their hearts thudded inside of their chests. They took a cautious step back. They wanted to open fire on him, but they feared he'd drop the grenade and blow all their asses up. "I don't see you popping all of that shit now! Now y'all scared! Yeah, yeah,yeah, look at all yo' pathetic asses! Either y'all let go of my boy or we all going up in here!"

"Yo', Cordell, what do we do now? This mothafucka kamikaze!" Savino said to his boss as he held his .9mm to the back of Tiaz' dome.

"Yeah, boss, this nigga'z loco, we should fall back!" One of the other men said.

"Nah, we not falling back for a goddamn thang," Cordell told his men. Although he was speaking to them, his eyes were focused on Melvin. "This asshole ain't gone do shit, as long as we have his boy. He loves him too much; I can see the shit all in his eyes. Ain't that right, Melvin? You love your boy, don't chu? You don't want anything to happen to him," he took a pull from his Black & Mild and blew out a smoke ring.

"Don't push me, man!" Melvin tilted his head to the side and looked at him like *I'm warning you, I'll do it.*

"You have been pushed. Now put the pin back into the grenade before I have Savino there put one in the back of your boy's thinking cap. You got until the count of three, and not a second more," he warned him as he continued to suck on the end of his Black & Mild and smoke wafted around him. "One..." he began his countdown.

"You think shit is a game, man? I'll blow us all to smithereens, play with me if you want to!"

"Two," Cordell said casually, keeping his eyes on Melvin. He carried on nonchalantly, as if he didn't have anything to worry about.

Melvin looked to his son. He could tell that he was fearful now, but he was still showing his heart like he always had.

"Do it, pop, do it! I ain't scared to die, I wanna see momma anyway." Tiaz told his father, looking him square in the eyes.

His heart was beating hard and he was nervous. But his old man had always told him to show his nuts when confronted with fear.

When Kimberly came to mind, Melvin realized then that he couldn't go through with his plans of suicide. He reminisced about the times he spent with his wife while she was pregnant. He also recalled his raising Tiaz from a baby to the teenage boy that he was today. It was at that time that he came to the conclusion that he couldn't set the grenade off.

"Three!"

"Wait! Hold up," Melvin raised his hand up to stop Savino from blowing Tiaz' head off, "I give up, I surrender." He held the grenade before Cordell's eyes and pushed the pin back into it. He then tossed it over to him. He caught it and tossed it up and down in his palm, treating it as if it were a baseball.

"Like I said, 'you love 'em too much,'"Cordell sat the grenade down on the coffee table and signaled his men over to Melvin. Melvin raised his hands into the air as the men approached him, holding up their AKs as they gripped them with both of their hands.

The first man to reach Melvin slammed the stock of his AK into his stomach, knocking the window out of him and doubling him over. Before he knew it, the other man that had approached with him, knocked him in his temple with the butt of his AK. The impact from the blow caused his eyes to roll into the back of his head. He went slamming to the floor on the side of his face. Seeing him barely conscious, the men kicked, stomped and slammed the butts of their assault rifles into his body violently.

"Leave 'em alone! Leave 'em alone, you bitch ass niggaz!" Tiaz hollered out to the men as they did a number on his father. He didn't dare to get up because Savino was still behind him and he knew that he wouldn't hesitate to pull the trigger.

While Melvin was getting the beating of his life, Cordell busied himself getting undressed. He removed his porkpie hat and his overcoat, lying them down on the arm of the couch. Bending down, he picked up a tool box and sat it down upon the coffee table. Opening it, he removed a hammer and a box of nails, which he smacked down on the coffee table beside the tool box. Next, he took out a roll of duct tape and sat it down beside the tool box.

"You're dead, all of you niggaz, you hear me? You're dead!" Tiaz promised with tears treading down his cheeks. It hurt him to see niggaz pummel his old man like that knowing that he was powerless to stop them.

"Didn't I tell you earlier to shut the fuck up, nigga?" Savino smacked him upside the back of the head with the butt of his .9mm again, lurching him forward. Tiaz winced and leaned his head aside. That's when Savino stepped in front of him and beat him in the face with the butt of his weapon, turning its handle crimson. "I bet cho ass won't say nothing else." Savino wiped the handle of his gun off with the end of Tiaz' shirt and stepped over to Melvin, getting his lick in on him as well.

"Alright, fellas, that's enough. Get 'em to his feet and plant 'em into a chair beside his kid," Cordell gave his men orders as he stood at the center of the floor holding a hammer and a box of nails. He watched as his men placed Melvin in a chair beside Tiaz. He then ordered them to duct tape him and his son's ankles to the legs of their respective chairs. Once they were done, he ordered them to turn on the stereo and hold Melvin's wrists down. With that having been done, Cordell stepped to his business. He sat the box of nails on Melvin's lap and took out a few nails. He placed a few of the nails into his mouth and placed one at the center of Melvin's hand.

Cordell was about to drive the first nail through Melvin's hand, but first, he looked up at him to see was he aware about what was going to take place. When he saw Melvin's eyes rolled to their whites and his head bobbing about, he concurred that he didn't have a clue as to what was about to happen. *Perfect!* Holding the nail against the center of Melvin's hand, Cordell raised his hammer and brought it down with all of his might.

*Cling!*

"Aahhhhh!" Melvin threw his head back and screamed aloud, showcasing all of the teeth inside of his mouth. His eyelids peeled far open from the sensational pain he was experiencing. *Cling!* "Aaahhhh!" *Cling! Cling! Cling!* "Aahhhh!" *Cling!*

Cordell stood up and tilted his head from side to side, taking in the first nail that he'd driven through Melvin's hand. Blood oozed out of the top of his hand where the wound was made and rolled between his fingers. The blood met underneath the armrest and dripped to the floor.

"Okay, on to the next one." Cordell pressed a nail against Melvin's other hand as he continued to holler out in pain in his ear. *Cling! Cling! Cling!* Melvin's eyelids eyes stretched further and further open with each strike of the hammer. He wailed at the top of his lungs, feeling the sharp nail being drove through his flesh. *Cling! Cling! Cling! Cling!*

Cordell stood back up after driving the nail through Melvin's other hand. He observed his handiwork and watched blood drip from the hand onto the floor. He then looked to Tiaz whose head was bowed. He could hear him moaning in pain from the beating he'd taken to the face by Savino's gun.

Cordell motioned for his men to hold down Tiaz' hands. They obliged him and he pressed a nail against the center of his hand. He lifted the hammer and brought it down with all of his might.

*Cling!*

"Aahhhhhhh!" Tiaz threw his head back hollering aloud. His eyelids were stretched wide open and his mouth was quaking from him hollering for so long.

\*\*\*

Melvin's eyelids flickered as he came back to his conscious state. He'd passed out earlier from his hands having been nailed to the armrest of the chair that he was sitting in. His hands were throbbing like a mothafucka from the nails that had been embedded in them.

Melvin's head bobbled about as he struggled to look around. He was seeing through blurred vision so he couldn't quite tell who it was standing before him. Once his vision did come into focus he saw that Cordell was standing on the side of his son, about to lift his .357 Magnum revolver. This scared the hell out of Melvin. His stomach twisted into knots and his heart pounded uncontrollably.

"Goddamn you, Cordell, don't chu kill my boy! Don't chu touch 'em!" Melvin shouted from the chair he was bounded to, spittle flying from his lips and his nostrils flaring. He tried to move, but his efforts were useless. His hands were nailed to the armrests of the chair and his ankles were duct-taped to its legs. Also, his face was bloody and bruised. His left eye was swollen shut while the right was narrowed from swelling. His broken nose was double in size and his busted lips caused him to talk funny.

Cordell held his silver .357 Magnum revolver against Tiaz' head causing it to bend at an angle. The boy had gotten his issue just as his old man had. His injuries mirrored his own. The blood that had ran from his face and down his neck had stained the collar of his wife beater pink. His eyes were staring out of their corners and his lips were a straight line.

He knew the risk of the deadly game he and his old man were playing, but he was still scared to die. His pop's made sure he was well aware of the graveyard risks they were taking and he agreed to go along with them.

With that in mind, Tiaz decided he wasn't about to tuck his nuts in the face of death. Nah, fuck that, he was going to let them hang.

Cordell looked from Tiaz to Melvin wearing a devilish grin as he held that steel to the side of his melon. He got a kick out of watching the older man beg for the life of his son.

"Now why wouldn't I kill this lil' mothafucka, huh? Tell me why?" His lips peeled back into a sneer. "Gemme one good goddamn reason. And maybe, just maybe I'll let 'em walk."

Melvin was quiet for a time as he looked away trying to conjure up a good enough reason to have his son exonerated.

"Welp," Cordell shrugged. "I guess this is goodbye, junior." He cocked the hammer of his revolver with his thumb and moved to squeeze the trigger.

"No! No! No! Wait!" Melvin shouted, seeing his son's brain about to get splattered.

"You better start doing a whole lotta talking real fast." Cordell's eyebrows arched and his nose scrunched as he gritted his teeth. Tiaz squeezed his eyelids closed tightly, waiting to be delivered to heaven or hell, whichever came first for people who'd done the dirt he'd done.

"The money, all of the money we've stole since we've been kickin' in does." Melvin spoke fast, hoping to change the course of his baby boy's fate.

"Money, huh? How much are we talking here?"

"Half—half a million dollars."

"Five hundred big ones, huh? I hear ya talking, but chu gone have to show me something." He put the hammer back into its rightful place and took the pistol away from Tiaz' temple causing him to sigh and relax. "I want that money right here and right now. So where is it?"

Melvin closed his eyes and swallowed, taking a deep breath, thanking the Lord for sparing his offspring. When he peeled his eyelids back open, he started rattling off the address where the money was hidden and where he'd stashed it.

Cordell sent his men after the loot. An hour later they returned with a Puma duffle bag. He ordered them to unzip the duffle bag and hold it open. When they did as instructed, his eyes were pleased by the contents inside. One of the henchmen zipped the duffle bag back up and dropped it at Cordell's feet.

"Now your end of the bargain." Melvin nodded to his boy, keeping his eyes on his abductor.

"Right. I am a man of my word." Cordell turned to one of his men. "Release the boy."

The henchman worked the nail back and forth with the hammer causing Tiaz to frown and clench his teeth, blood splattered on the scratched up hardwood floor creating a small pool.

*Snikt! Thump! Snikt! Thump!*

The nails made their noise as they dropped to the floor, stained with blood. The henchman kneeled to the floor, sitting the hammer down and unsheathing a knife. He sliced the duct-tape around the boy's ankles and snatched it loose.

Tiaz rose to his feet wincing as he looked at his wounded hands. He quickly forgot about them when he realized his father hadn't been set free, yet. He ran towards him but Cordell stepped in his path. He stared up at him like, *Get the fuck out of my way or get your ass bowled over.*

"Give us a minute, please." Melvin asked of Cordell and he moved from the young nigga'z path. "Come here, son." He winced, aching from the injuries to his hands and face. His boy stepped before him. "Get outta here, son."

"Pop, I'm not leaving here without you. Fuck these niggaz." He mad dogged all of the opposing men in the room, then he looked back to his father.

"Listen, you gotta get outta here now. If you don't, we're both dead. Please."

There was silence as father and son stared into one another's faces, their eyes saying what their mouths hadn't the courage to mention. Melvin hadn't been too big on affection with his first born, so he let his actions show him what he couldn't verbalize.

"I love you, son." Melvin told his son for the first time ever in his entire life. Although the young nigga hated to have to hear it at a time like this, he realized that it was better hearing it now then to never have heard it all.

Those words made Tiaz' eyes turn glassy, but he refused to shed a tear in front of the men present. Without saying a word, he wrapped his arms around his old man firmly. His father kissed him on the cheek and the side of the head.

"Go, son, go! Get outta here." Melvin threw his head towards the door.

"I love you too, pop."

"I know. Now gone son, get!"

Tiaz headed for the door, glaring at the henchmen as he went along. He stopped at the one that had just opened the door for him, hocking up spit and hawking it into his face. The man closed his eyes and brought the end of his bandana up to his face, wiping his face clean. Tiaz crossed the threshold out of the door. Going down the steps he heard the muffled commotion coming from inside of the house he'd just left.

"It's time to pay your tithes, Mel." He barely heard Cordell say.

"Ol' Melvin Petty has always been good for it. I always pay my debts."

"And that's why I fucks with chu."

"You just remember when it's all said and done, they gone bury me a G, you hear me? Bury me a mothafucking G! A G! A…"

*Bop! Bop! Bop! Bop!*

Once the shots went off, Tiaz closed his eyelids and tears shot down his cheeks. He never broke his stride as he headed out of the front yard of the house.

Tiaz was sure of one thing at that moment; he wouldn't rest until he avenged his father's murder. With the assistance of Threat, he was going to track down all parties involved. His execution of them was going to be swift and carried out with extreme prejudice.

Tranay Adams

## CHAPTER TWENTY-ONE

Tiaz climbed in behind the wheel of his father's car. He then tore off lengths of the fabric of his wife beater, tying them around his wounded hands. It took him some time to tighten the rags around his hands being that they were extremely sore and aching, but he finally managed. He had to hotwire the vehicle since he didn't have the keys, but even that proved to be difficult due to his hands.

Tiaz tried to grip the steering wheel of the automobile, so he could back out of the space, but he couldn't manage to do so. His hands had proven to be his handicap. Giving up, he threw open the door and hopped out. He found himself running down the sidewalk, as fast as he could. Occasionally, he'd glance over his shoulder to see if Cordell and his men were following him, but they weren't anywhere in sight. Before Tiaz knew it, he had made it to his destination, which was Threat's house.

***

Breathing heavily, Tiaz made it to the backyard of Threat's house. Looking in through the window, all he could see were the ruined white blinds. Some of them were broken off at their corners. He believed that this was from his homeboy peering out into his backyard to see what was going on inside of the alley. Through the broken off parts of the blinds, Tiaz could see that the bedroom was dark, but he saw flashes of blue light, which he gathered was the television set.

Raising his fist, Tiaz knocked on the window and waited for his homeboy to answer him. He looked over his shoulders and ran over to the gate that led to the backyard to see if anyone had followed him. For some strange reason he had the feeling that Cordell would change his mind and send his men to shoot him down like a dog in the streets.

Hearing the window being opened, Tiaz ran back to it, just in time to see Threat sticking his head out. He was bare chest and wearing brown Dickie's shorts which sagged off his ass and showing off his boxers. His face was fixed with a frown and his gun was in his hand.

Tiaz, is that chu?" Threat narrowed his eyelids trying to see through the darkness. He garnered that it was his partner in crime from the outlining of his body.

"Yeah, it's me, Crim." Tiaz said, the pain in his voice was evident. He tried to mask it, but he couldn't help it.

"Thought chu was an enemy or some shit, homeboy. I was about to start…" his words died in his throat when he saw his right-hand man's bruised and battered face as well as his rag tied hands. "Aww, not my nigga! What happened to you? Who did this to you, homie?" Threat tucked his gun at the small of his back and grabbed the pane of the window, hopping out of it. He landed to the ground on his bending knees and rose to his feet. He grabbed Tiaz by his shoulders and looked into his face. His tearing eyes twinkled in the dim lighting that the light posts out in the alley provided.

"They killed 'em, they killed 'em." Tiaz broke down crying, tears sliding down his cheeks. His shoulders rocked and his hands trembled. Usually, Tiaz was the pillar of strength and checked his emotions. Under no circumstances would he ever want anyone to see him like he was now. His being this way would have someone thinking that he was weak, and he couldn't have that. This was because his reputation was everything to him. As of now, his street credibility didn't mean shit to him; he'd just lost his father. His old man was the only man on this God forsaken planet that he'd ever loved, besides his homeboy, Threat.

"Who, nigga? Who are you talking about?" Threat frowned as he shook his main man trying to get the answer out of him.

"Cordell. Cordell, Savino, and the rest of them niggaz under his thumb," Tiaz sniffled and wiped his tears with the back of his hand. Bringing his head back up, he looked Threat directly in the eyes. "I swear 'fore God, Threat. Once I heal up, I'm gonna kill every last one of them niggaz! Fuck 'em all. I'm not sparing a soul, on my momma's grave. You feel me?"

"I feel you, homeboy. And I'ma ride witchu when you ready to roll."

"Thanks." Tiaz used the lower half of his wife beater to wipe his face.

Threat gripped his main man's shoulder and looked him in his eyes. "You straight, homie?"

"Nah, I'm fucked up, homeboy, but I will be in time. At least I hope so," he admitted.

"You can stay here as long as you want. I'm sure my granny won't mind once I tell her what's up."

"Good looking out, that's love."

"No doubt."

"I'm strapped out here, Crim. I ain't got no fam or nothing. A nigga broke."

"Look at me, homie, look me dead in my mothafucking eyes," he began, keeping eye contact with Tiaz. "As long as this lil' nigga breathing, you always got family. I am your brother. Whatever I have is half yours. Long as I got it, you got it. That's how it works with family. You hear me?" Tiaz nodded. "I love you, my nigga, and we gone lay all of these busta ass niggaz down 'cause the nigga that they took wasn't just yo' father, he was mine, too."

At that moment, Tiaz embraced Threat like a brother. They stood where they were locked in the moment. What

Threat had said made Tiaz feel a little better, but once he got his revenge, he'd feel a lot better.

"I love you, bruh." Tiaz said to him.

"I love you too, homeboy, you my mothafucking nigga. Straight up," he kissed him on the side of the head.

\*\*\*

### Ten months later

Cordell sat at the head of a table inside of a restaurant known as Elegance. The upscale establishment was widely known for its food, music, entertainment and service. They were pretty well rounded as far as cuisines were concerned, but they specialized in Italian entrées. If you wanted some good Italian food, Elegance was definitely the place you'd want to try. Anyway, tonight was a special night. You see, Cordell had just closed a deal on some of the sweetest cocaine money could buy from his new plug, Black Jesus. So he'd gathered all of his lieutenants to personally thank them for helping him build his empire and give them a gift.

Cordell and his lieutenants finished eating their food and wiped their mouths with their cloth napkin. As soon as they'd done this, the last person on duty, the chef, pushed out a cart occupied by silver platters with bubble lids. The chef sat a platter each before the men sitting at the table. He then approached Cordell who reached inside of his suit and pulled out a hefty envelope. He passed it to the chef and he thanked him, sliding the envelope inside of his uniform. The man went into the back where he changed out of his uniform and headed out of the door.

"What's this, boss man?" Savino asked, looking back and forth from the silver bubble lid on his platter to the nigga whose employ he was under. It had taken some time but Cordell was finally able to convince his thuggish ass to put on a suit for the occasion. The mothafucka had planned on showing up in a Dickie suit and Chuck Taylor's, but thankfully his boss was able to persuade him.

"Just my way of thanking each and every last one of you niggaz here at this table for helping me build and establish this empire of mine," he stopped a wine glass at his lips. "Y'all gone ahead and take a peek." He took a sip of the wine, savoring its expensive taste before swallowing.

Although Cordell was in a suit, he also wore a gold crown and a gold saucer sized medallion and several icy gold rings. He claimed to be The King of the Steets, so he dressed himself up to look like royalty, street royalty, as far as jewels were concerned.

*Cliiing! Cliiing! Cliiing! Cliiing! Cliiing!*

The men sitting at the table pulled off the silver bubble lids, one by one. Sitting on the platters before him were small black jewelry boxes labeled Rolex in gold with a matching crown above it. Smirks appeared on Savino and the men's faces when they saw the boxes with the gold letters on them. Gently, they opened the boxes and revealed their respective watches. All of the watches were different, but they all were beautifully crafted and one of its kind.

Cordell smiled from ear to ear seeing his men happily sliding on the Rolexes that he'd bought them. He observed them holding up their wrist to their faces and twisting and turning the watch adorning their wrist.

"Good lookin' out, Cordell." Savino said.

"Appreciate this, boss dawg, this watch hard as a mothafucka!" Another one of the men stated. The rest of the men gave Cordell their praise and thanks, as they admired their watches.

"Don't mention it. Y'all niggaz stick with me, and next time I'm gonna be giving you keys to Ferraris and shit. Watch and see what loyalty, dedication and determination gets you," he went to take another sip of wine, and a car alarm sounded from outside in the parking lot. He sat the glass down and looked through the large picturesque window. He could see the headlights of his Mercedes Benz 600 Flashing on and off, as the vehicle's alarm blared loudly. "Shit."

"That's you, Cordell? I thought that was my shit." One of the lieutenants said. He'd just put his car keys back inside of his pocket.

"Yeah, that's me." Cordell confirmed. He'd pulled out his car keys and turned the alarm off. When he went to take a sip of wine, the alarm sounded again and he turned it off. It came on again and that's when he rose from the table, adjusting his leather belt. "You, gentlemen, have to excuse me, but I gotta check on my car. It must be faulty wiring or something that keeps this mothafucka going off," he walked off talking under his breath. "Mercedes...top of the line my ass. As much money as I paid for this fucking car, you'd think the goddamn alarm system would at least be in working order."

Cordell pushed open the door as he crossed the threshold out of Elegance. He made his way toward his car with his hands inside of his slacks. His alarm went off again and the headlights of his Benz flashed on and off again. He scowled, shook his head and cursed under his breath.

"Fuck that! I'm taking this son of a bitch back. They'd just gone have to give a nigga a new one." Cordell went to pull his keys out of his pocket when the restaurant suddenly exploded. The force behind the blast sent Cordell flying through the air and crashing down on the hood of an X5 truck. He rolled off the hood and smacked down on the surface.

As soon as the restaurant exploded, fire balls and broken glass came erupting out of all the windows of the establishment. Severed arms, legs, torsos and heads came along too. Some of the body parts landed on the windshields of parked cars, cracking their glass into cobwebs. While others smacked up against the backseat windows of vehicles and cracked the windows. Other body parts, which were burning, landed on the ground.

"Uhhh," Cordell struggled to lift his head up, looking through narrowed eyelids at the burning restaurant. His blurring vision went in and out. Suddenly, his head smacked down to the ground. He lay where he was unconscious.

The golden orange flames of the fire that was devouring what was left of Elegance illuminated Cordell's form as he lay flat on the ground. The light of the fire shining on him cast his shadow on the asphalt that was the parking lot grounds.

For a minute there wasn't any sound besides the crackling of the flames of the fire. Then Tiaz approached and stopped before Cordell, staring down at him with hatred in his eyes. Down at his side, his healed, scared hand, held on to a detonator. He hocked up phlegm and spit on Cordell. As soon as he did, a brown El Camino with shiny chrome rims stopped beside Tiaz. When he looked up, he found Chief hanging out of the driver side window, one hand gripping the steering wheel.

"We straight?" Chief asked.

"Yeah, we good," Tiaz tapped his fist against his chest.

"Alright then, I'm outty five thousand," Chief threw up his hand and peeled off. Chief was the chef that had sat out all of the silver bubble lid platters before Cordell's lieutenants and left the push cart behind. On that pushcart, beneath the white cloth, was a C4 explosive. This explosive was set off by Tiaz.

Chief was the cat that had met Melvin back at The Bar Fly and hired him to kill J-Murda who had been carrying on an affair with his wife. The contract was filled and

Melvin was paid. But the men kept in contact in case Chief decided to have his wife murdered. If the child she was pregnant with wasn't his then Chief would pay to have his wife knocked off as well.

Once the baby was born Chief found out that the child wasn't of his bloodline. It was then that he called Tiaz to whack out his wife. Having lost his mother as he was born, Tiaz couldn't bring himself to cap off Chief's wife so he tapped Threat to step in. The little nigga handled his business, but Tiaz didn't want money. This was because Tiaz learned that Chief was the chef at Elegance, Cordell's restaurant, and he wanted to enlist his help in exchange for the murder of the man's wife. The favor was for him to roll the push cart of explosives out into the dining room, which he did. All he had to do after that was leave and stay until the kills had been confirmed.

Tiaz looked on as Chief pulled out of the parking lot and made a right. As he went down the street and disappeared from out of his sight, the young nigga pulled out a detonator and pressed the button on it. Instantly, a loud explosion shook the ground and a flash of light illuminated the sky as a fireball shot up into the air. The sound of the explosion was so great that it set off the alarms of the nearby vehicles aligning the street.

"Rest in peace, godfather," Tiaz said as he looked up into the sky and crossed himself in the sign of the crucifix. Chief was the correctional officer that was giving Tiaz, Melvin's best friend, a hard time while he was on lock. He had put a hit out on Tiaz because he'd turned down his sexual advances. You see, Chief was bi-sexual. He liked pussy and dick. He'd taken a liking to Tiaz and wanted to run up in him, but homeboy didn't get down like that. The nigga felt embarrassed and humiliated when Tiaz shot him down, so he went ahead and put in the order to have him murdered.

*Bloc!*

Tiaz ducked feeling something hot whiz past his ear. Stooping low, he turned around and looked to the burning establishment. A smoking Savino stood inside of the doorway of the restaurant, pointing his wafting gun at Tiaz. Half of his face was charred and his right eye had discoloration from the explosion. His suit had been burned so badly that half of it clung to his burned flesh like a second skin.

*Bloc! Bloc! Bloc!*

Tiaz ducked and ran out of the way of the gunfire and pulled out his Beretta. He stooped low beside a parked BMW and peered up through its driver side window. He was just in time to see Threat running up on Savino, squeezing off. The man's body jerked from each bullet he took until he eventually fell over with his legs going up in the air. Savino tried to rise from where he had fallen to recover his gun, but the little nigga ran up on him, giving it to him all in his mothafucking chest.

*Poc! Poc! Poc! Poc! Poc!*

"I got the crown now, bitch!" Threat spoke of the imaginary crown of the hardest nigga in the streets him and Savino had been beefing over. He then lowered his smoking gun to his side, having finished off Savino and taken a deep breath. It was almost over. One more nigga to go and Tiaz would finally have his revenge. Looking over his shoulder, Threat saw Tiaz motion him over with his gun. He came running over to him looking around to make sure no one was watching them. Although he didn't see anyone, he could hear police sirens and fire trucks rushing to their location.

Threat jogged to a stop once he'd reached his crime partner. He breathed a little heavier than usual from the run.

"We gotta get up outta here 'fore The Ones turn out, Crim. Help me get this sack of shit inside of the trunk so we can roll out." Tiaz told him. Threat nodded and tucked his gun at the small of his back. He then popped the trunk of his father's Chevrolet Caprice. He and Tiaz grabbed an unconscious Cordell under either of his arms and dragged his ass over to the trunk. On the count of three, they grunted and hoisted his ass over inside of the trunk. Threat shut the trunk closed and ran over to the driver's door. He hopped in behind the wheel and cranked the hood classic up. Once Tiaz had pulled his leg inside of the automobile and slammed the door shut, he pulled out of the parking lot and into the street. Adjusting his rearview mirror, he looked up into it and saw the burning restaurant in the background. He also saw the red and blue lights of approaching police cars and the red lights of fire trucks.

## CHAPTER TWENTY-TWO

Tiaz rode shotgun in the Chevrolet looking at the wounds at the center of his palms he'd gotten the night Cordell nailed his hands to the armrest of his chair. The scars that the wounds left behind felt funny and every time it was really cold or raining outside his hands would ache.

Threat looked back and forth between the windshield and Tiaz. A frown was on his face as he wondered if his right-hand man was okay.

"You good, my nigga?" Threat questioned with concern.

Tiaz dropped his hands into his lap and said, "Yeah, I'm straight. We almost there?" He asked him.

"Yeah, in about ten mo'…" Threat's words died in his throat once he heard bumping around inside of the trunk. Tiaz went to say something and he held up his hand, stopping him. "You hear that?"

Tiaz sat where he was quiet trying to listen for the noise again. *Bump! Bump! Bump! Bump!* The pounding grew louder and more aggressive.

"Yeah, I hear it. That's that bitch ass nigga banging around inside of the trunk," Tiaz' face twisted and his nostrils flared. "Yo', homeboy, calm that shit down in there, 'fore I have the homie pull this bitch over!"

*Bump! Bump! Bump! Bump!*

"That's it. Pull this mothafucka over! This nigga thinks I'm bullshitting with his ass."

"Alright," Threat told him, putting on his right turn signal and pulling over to a dark area of the road. In a flash, Tiaz hopped out of the car and headed to the rear of it. He knocked on the trunk and his homeboy popped it open.

"Fuck I tell you, huh?" Tiaz leaned over inside of the trunk, repeatedly punching Cordell in the face until he was breathing out of breath. Grabbing hold of the trunk, he lifted his foot and stomped him out furiously. He then spit on him and slammed the trunk back shut, walking around the car to get back into the front passenger seat, breathing hard. He told his right-hand man to drive off and he did.

"You good, Crim?" Threat inquired, seeing the blood on his knuckles.

"Yeah, I'm straight." He let the window down and threw out the balled up napkin he'd taken out of the glove-box to wipe the blood off his knuckles. The balled up napkin hit the ground and tumbled a little before settling. Tiaz then let the window back up. "This is it coming up ahead," he pointed with his finger.

Threat made a left off the road and into the woods, rolling over twigs and brittle leaves hearing them crunching and snapping beneath the chrome rims and tires of the Chevy Caprice. The only thing that could be seen was the red brakes lights at the back of the car as it traveled through the darkness. The Chevy Caprice stopped. Threat and Tiaz hopped out, making their way to the trunk of the vehicle. They opened the trunk and for the first time, Threat saw Cordell after Tiaz had worked him over during their last stop. Cordell's right eye was swollen with a bluish black ring underneath it. His nose was fractured and bleeding. There was also speckles of blood on his suit.

"Alright, homeboy, get cho punk ass out the trunk," Tiaz and Threat grabbed Cordell under either of his arms and hoisted him out of the trunk. When they took him out he nearly fell. His legs felt like cooked noodles underneath him and he was having trouble standing. This was because his legs had fallen asleep during the long drive over to the location. Still, that didn't stop the young niggaz from helping him over to the front of the Caprice. The headlights of the classic vehicle were shining, illuminating what was a six foot deep hole in the ground. Beside the hole there was a shovel standing straight up in a pile of dirt the color of coffee beans. When Cordell seen the hole his eyes bulged and his head whipped back and forth between Threat and Tiaz. He hollered out disrespectful shit at the young men. He struggled to get loose from their grips, turning from left to right violently, but never breaking free. Seeing that his efforts were useless, he decided to try a different approach to the situation. Abruptly, he slumped and allowed his knees to be dragged through the dirt and leaves, dirtying the knees of his slacks. The dead weight did little to stop Threat and Tiaz from pulling him along. He made their job harder, but they hoisted his ass back up by his arms and kept moving forward with him.

"Fuck this, I'm not finna keep dragging this bitch ass nigga along," Threat wiped his shiny forehead with the back of his hand. He then looked at his hand and saw that it was wet from his perspiration. "Gotta nigga out here sweating and shit." In a flash, Threat whipped out his .45 automatic and pressed it into Cordell's crotch. "Check this out, my nigga, you gone get cho ass up and walk over to this hole or I'ma shoot cho mothafucking balls off. That's on everything," he scowled and clenched his jaws, showcasing the skeletal bone structure in his face.

Cordell shut his eyelids briefly and took a deep breath. He then climbed up on his feet, standing tall. Threat tucked his banga on his waistline and punched Cordell in his stomach, knocking the wind out of him. The blow caused his eyes to bulge and him to double over in pain.

"That's for making me break a sweat out this mothafucka," he hooked his arm with the crack king's and then said, "Now, bring yo' ass on!"

Threat and Tiaz walked the crack king over to the pre-dug grave. They turned him around so that his back was at the six feet hole and he was facing them. Tiaz then went to stand beside Threat, and they pulled out their respective guns. Afterwards, they turned their hateful eyes on the man that had ordered Melvin's death, trigger fingers itching.

"Any last words, ol' hoe ass nigga?" Tiaz asked. Although he hated the nigga'z guts, he was still going to give him the respect of reciting his last words.

"Yeah," Cordell nodded, "Yeah, I got some last words, fight me, goddamn it! Fight me right here and right now! Any nigga can pick up a gun and pop something! But it takes a real man to go from the shoulders and throw them mothafucking hands. You feel me, huh?" The crack king stared Tiaz in his eyes, hoping he'd go for the bait he'd cast out on the line.

Tiaz and Threat exchanged glances.

"You tryna squabble this fool?" Threat asked him in a hushed tone.

"Yeah, I can take 'em." Tiaz looked from his homeboy to Cordell. "I'ma beat the brakes offa his mothafucking ass."

"Take me? Take this nigga standing before you?" Cordell looked at him like he must have been crazy thinking that he could stand a chance against him. "Boy, you must have slipped, fell, and bumped yo' mothafucking head. Shiiiit, you better ask somebody 'bout this one right here. My knuckle game heard 'round the city! If I ain't known for nothing else it's putting lil' punk ass niggaz like you on they backs, ya understand me, you lil' mothafucka you?" He spat on the ground and allowed what he had said to marinate in Tiaz' brain. He only hoped that the young nigga'z pride would get the best of him and he'd give him that fair one he was looking for.

"Hold this," Tiaz passed Threat his gun.

"Yeaaah, that's what I'm talking about, baby. Come on and get this ass whipping." Cordell licked his lips and smiled wickedly.

"Fuck this nigga, man, don't let 'em get in yo' head. Let's blast his ass, bury him, and bounce back to the hood." Threat tried to reason as he held a gun on either side of him.

"Nah, Crim, I'ma show this fool how niggaz from the set give it up. You feel me?" Tiaz pulled his shirt from over his head and tossed it upon the hood of the Caprice.

Threat looked back and forth between his homeboy and Cordell. He saw in the older man's face that he really thought that he could whip his right-hand man's ass. That really made him want to see his comrade beat the old head's ass.

"Fuck this nigga, T, beat his ass, homeboy." Threat egged his brother from another on.

"That's the plan, Stan."Tiaz replied, pulling his belt tighter on his waist and then buckling it. He then pulled the orange bandana from out of his back pocket and drew Threat's from his back pocket. "Lace me up, my nigga."

"Fa sho'," Threat tucked the burners on him and began tying the bandanas around his homeboy's fists. While he was doing this, Tiaz was mad dogging Cordell. The older man's head was tilted down and he was glaring up at him threateningly, jaws clenched so tight that his bone structure was shown in them.

"What we playing for, OG?" Tiaz inquired.

"Blood," Cordell replied.

"Good enough for me," he cracked a smirk as Threat tied the last bandana around his fist. He then went to wiggle his fingers and cracked his knuckles.

"Y'all two niggaz can play for blood, but I want that chain around his neck," Threat pulled out his guns and pointed one of them at the gold chain holding the saucer sized medallion around the crack king's neck. "We can get a lil' wager going. You put hands on the homie and you walk outta here; you don't, and the chain is mine, deal?"

"You got it," Cordell answered, keeping his glare on Tiaz. They were mad dogging one another unflinchingly.

"Alright then," Threat turned to face his comrade, giving the crack king his back. "Gone and fade this nigga. Even if you do lose, I'ma pop his ass and we still gone walk off victorious."

"Nah, homeboy, if I lose, you let old head walk. That's the deal, no sucker shit. We stand-up niggaz, we live by our word. You hear me?" Tiaz asked, looking his best friend in the eyes. "Even if I lose, you let 'em walk. You got that, my nigga?" Threat nodded. "Then let me hear you say it then."

"Even if you do lose, let old head walk." Threat repeated what he had been told.

"Good. Now, let's get this mothafucka cracking." Tiaz teetered from foot to foot and started shadow boxing. His fists were coming out so fast that they looked like blurs.

Threat stepped over to the Caprice and opened the driver's door. He sat down on the seat and stuck his head outside the door, saying, "Alright, I'ma shut these lights off, when they come back on, y'all niggaz do yo' shit."

While he was talking, Cordell was shadow boxing as well. Finishing up, he stepped before Tiaz who was stretching his limbs. The older man did the same, preparing himself for the fight. Once they were done prepping, they stood before one another with their dukes up.

Threat's eyes stayed on them as he brought his hand to the switch that operated the headlights of the hood classic.

*I should have my fucking head examined going along with this shit. We shoulda just peeled this nigga'z cap back and dropped his ass in that hole so we could bury 'em and get the fuck on,* Threat thought and shook his head. He was always letting Tiaz' talk him into doing shit he didn't really want any parts of. *Fuck it! That's my nigga and I'ma right 'til the death of me. If this is what he wants then let's get to it then!*

Threat flipped the switch and the lights went out, leaving them in complete darkness. It was pretty much quiet that night besides the hoots of an owl. Suddenly, the headlights came back on and shined on Tiaz and Cordell. The illumination of the twin orbs made them appear as silhouettes moving before the Caprice.

Cordell attacked Tiaz with finesse and vigor. He gave him two haymakers to the face that whipped his head from left to right. He then followed up with an uppercut that sent his young ass stumbling backwards in a hurry. Tiaz fell up against the grill of the Chevy and bumped the back of his head, grimacing. When he peeled his eyelids back open, he saw the bottom of his rival's dress shoe flying at him, full speed ahead. He moved his head to the left at the last minute and the man's shoe got caught inside of the custom grill of the vehicle. He winced as he repeatedly tried to yank it free, but it wouldn't budge. Tiaz came back up and punched him in the crotch, causing him to throw his head back and howl in pain, grabbing between his legs.

When he did this, Tiaz hopped upon his feet and rushed him. He lifted him up off of his feet and charged forward, slamming him into a tree. The impact from the collision caused brittle leaves to fall from off the branches. Tiaz pulled back from off his rival and gave him body shots. The back to back blows doubled Cordell's over and he grabbed his sides. Abruptly, he clapped Tiaz' ears and caused them to ring with an eerie siren. The young man staggered backwards holding his ears and wincing. When he looked back up, Cordell snatched up a big ass crooked branch and swung it at his head. Tiaz ducked it, and when he came back up, he found himself having to dodge wild swings of the branch. He dodged the last swing of the branch by bending backwards. Once he came back up, he kicked the dirt and sent some smacking into Cordell's face, burning his eyes like mace. The crack king hollered out and tried to get the stuff from out of his eyes. That's when Tiaz rushed and tackled him to the ground. Once he had him on his back, he pinned his arms down with his knees and rose up. He stared down at his face and clutched his fists tightly. His fists went one after another, slamming into Cordell's face, rearranging his bone structure and bruising him. Tiaz didn't stop until he was exhausted and his upper half was glistening from sweat. Looking down, he saw that Cordell's face was bloody and swollen. His right eye was bloodshot and his nose was twice its size. A mouthful of blood left his teeth red. His jaw was broken so his mouth was moving like a fish out of water.

"That's it, that's what I'm talking about, my nigga, you whipped that ass!" Threat jumped for joy and swung on the air.

Tiaz wiped his forehead with the back of his hand and stood to his feet. He grabbed Cordell by the back of his shirt with one hand and pulled him towards the grave he'd personally dug. He breathed heavily, chest leaping up and down, as he dragged his defeated foe over to the six foot plot. Afterwards, he snatched the gold chain from around his neck and tossed it over to Threat. Once the shorter man caught the chain, he held it up around his neck to see how it would look on him.

While he was doing that, Tiaz snatched the shovel out of the pile of dirt and stepped to his business, which was burying that cock sucker, Cordell.

Threat stashed the chain inside of his pocket and placed his hand on his comrade's shoulder. "You okay, my nigga?"

"I'm straight, homeboy. I told you I was gone spank that ass, didn't I?" Tiaz began shoveling dirt into the grave. The dirt crashed on top of Cordell's chest and slid underneath his chin. The crack king turned his head from left to right, moving his mouth animatedly.

"Sho' did," Threat agreed, smiling and dapping him up. He then grabbed the other shovel which was lying on the opposite side of the pre-dug grave and assisted his homie in burying Cordell.

"Gaaagh!" Cordell gagged and coughed on the dirt that landed inside of his mouth. Half of it was covering his face and the upper half of body. He spat some of the dirt out, but there was still some inside of his mouth. All he could hear were the grunts of the young niggaz as their shovels hit the land, scooping up piles of it. Then there was the sound of the dirt smacking down upon his submerged form inside of the grave. As he listened to these continuous noises, he called out as best as he could with a broken jaw, "Bury me a G! Bury me a G! Bury me a mothafucking G!

**THE END**

# Submission Guideline

Submit the first three chapters of your completed manuscript to ldpsubmissions@gmail.com, subject line: Your book's title. The manuscript must be in a .doc file and sent as an attachment. Document should be in Times New Roman, double spaced and in size 12 font. Also, provide your synopsis and full contact information. If sending multiple submissions, they must each be in a separate email.

Have a story but no way to send it electronically? You can still submit to LDP/Ca$h Presents. Send in the first three chapters, written or typed, of your completed manuscript to:

**LDP: Submissions Dept**
**Po Box 870494**
**Mesquite, Tx 75187**

*DO NOT send original manuscript. Must be a duplicate.*

Provide your synopsis and a cover letter containing your full contact information.

Thanks for considering LDP and Ca$h Presents.

BOW DOWN TO MY GANGSTA

By **Ca$h**

TORN BETWEEN TWO

By **Coffee**

BLOOD STAINS OF A SHOTTA **III**

By **Jamaica**

STEADY MOBBIN **III**

By **Marcellus Allen**

BLOOD OF A BOSS **V**

By **Askari**

LOYAL TO THE GAME **IV**

LIFE OF SIN II

By **T.J. & Jelissa**

A DOPEBOY'S PRAYER **II**

By **Eddie "Wolf" Lee**

IF LOVING YOU IS WRONG… **III**

LOVE ME EVEN WHEN IT HURTS **II**

By **Jelissa**

TRUE SAVAGE **VII**

By **Chris Green**

BLAST FOR ME **III**

A BRONX TALE III

DUFFLE BAG CARTEL

By **Ghost**

ADDICTIED TO THE DRAMA **III**

By **Jamila Mathis**

LIPSTICK KILLAH **III**

Tranay Adams

WHAT BAD BITCHES DO **III**

KILL ZONE **II**

By **Aryanna**

THE COST OF LOYALTY **II**

By **Kweli**

SHE FELL IN LOVE WITH A REAL ONE **II**

By **Tamara Butler**

RENEGADE BOYS **III**

By **Meesha**

CORRUPTED BY A GANGSTA **IV**

By **Destiny Skai**

A GANGSTER'S CODE **III**

By **J-Blunt**

KING OF NEW YORK IV

RISE TO POWER II

By **T.J. Edwards**

GORILLAS IN THE BAY II

**De'Kari**

THE STREETS ARE CALLING II

**Duquie Wilson**

KINGPIN KILLAZ III

**Hood Rich**

STEADY MOBBIN' **III**

**Marcellus Allen**

SINS OF A HUSTLA II

**ASAD**

TRIGGADALE II

**Elijah R. Freeman**

MARRIED TO A BOSS 2…

**By Destiny Skai & Chris Green**

KINGS OF THE GAME II

**Playa Ray**


<u>**Available Now**</u>

<u>RESTRAINING ORDER **I & II**</u>

By **CA$H & Coffee**

<u>LOVE KNOWS NO BOUNDARIES **I II & III**</u>

By **Coffee**

<u>RAISED AS A GOON I, II, III & IV</u>

<u>BRED BY THE SLUMS I, II, III</u>

<u>BLAST FOR ME I & II</u>

<u>ROTTEN TO THE CORE I III</u>

<u>A BRONX TALE I, II</u>

By **Ghost**

<u>LAY IT DOWN **I & II**</u>

<u>LAST OF A DYING BREED</u>

<u>BLOOD STAINS OF A SHOTTA I & II</u>

By **Jamaica**

<u>LOYAL TO THE GAME</u>

<u>LOYAL TO THE GAME II</u>

<u>LOYAL TO THE GAME III</u>

<u>LIFE OF SIN</u>

By **TJ & Jelissa**

<u>BLOODY COMMAS I & II</u>

<u>SKI MASK CARTEL I II & III</u>

Tranay Adams

KING OF NEW YORK I II,III

RISE TO POWER

By **T.J. Edwards**

IF LOVING HIM IS WRONG…I & II

LOVE ME EVEN WHEN IT HURTS

By **Jelissa**

WHEN THE STREETS CLAP BACK I & II III

By **Jibril Williams**

A DISTINGUISHED THUG STOLE MY HEART I II & III

LOVE SHOULDN'T HURT I II III

RENEGADE BOYS I & II

By **Meesha**

A GANGSTER'S CODE I & II

**By J-Blunt**

By **Bre' Hayes**

BLOOD OF A BOSS **I, II, III & IV**

By **Askari**

THE STREETS BLEED MURDER **I, II & III**

THE HEART OF A GANGSTA I II& III

By **Jerry Jackson**

CUM FOR ME

CUM FOR ME 2

CUM FOR ME 3

CUM FOR ME 4

An **LDP Erotica Collaboration**

BRIDE OF A HUSTLA **I II & II**

THE FETTI GIRLS **I, II& III**

CORRUPTED BY A GANGSTA I, II & III

By **Destiny Skai**

WHEN A GOOD GIRL GOES BAD

By **Adrienne**

A GANGSTER'S REVENGE **I II III & IV**

THE BOSS MAN'S DAUGHTERS

THE BOSS MAN'S DAUGHTERS II

THE BOSSMAN'S DAUGHTERS III

THE BOSSMAN'S DAUGHTERS IV

THE BOSS MAN'S DAUGHTERS **V**

A SAVAGE LOVE **I & II**

BAE BELONGS TO ME

A HUSTLER'S DECEIT I, II

WHAT BAD BITCHES DO I, II

By **Aryanna**

A KINGPIN'S AMBITON

A KINGPIN'S AMBITION **II**

I MURDER FOR THE DOUGH

By **Ambitious**

TRUE SAVAGE

TRUE SAVAGE II

TRUE SAVAGE **III**

TRUE SAVAGE **IV**

TRUE SAVAGE **V**

TRUE SAVAGE **VI**

By **Chris Green**

A DOPEBOY'S PRAYER

By **Eddie "Wolf" Lee**

THE KING CARTEL **I, II & III**

By **Frank Gresham**

THESE NIGGAS AIN'T LOYAL **I, II & III**

By **Nikki Tee**


By **CATO**


By **Phoenix**

BOSS'N UP **I , II & III**

By **Royal Nicole**

I LOVE YOU TO DEATH

**By Destiny J**

I RIDE FOR MY HITTA

I STILL RIDE FOR MY HITTA

By **Misty Holt**


By **Qay Crockett**


**SINS OF A HUSTLA**

By **ASAD**

BROOKLYN HUSTLAZ

By **Boogsy Morina**

BROOKLYN ON LOCK I & II

By **Sonovia**

GANGSTA CITY

By **Teddy Duke**

A DRUG KING AND HIS DIAMOND I & II III

A DOPEMAN'S RICHES

HER MAN, MINE'S TOO I, II

CASH MONEY HO'S

**By Nicole Goosby**

TRAPHOUSE KING **I II & III**

KINGPIN KILLAZ

By **Hood Rich**

LIPSTICK KILLAH **I, II**

CRIME OF PASSION I & II

By **Mimi**

STEADY MOBBN' **I, II**

By **Marcellus Allen**

WHO SHOT YA **I, II**

**Renta**

GORILLAZ IN THE BAY

**DE'KARI**

TRIGGADALE

**Elijah R. Freeman**

GOD BLESS THE TRAPPERS I, II, III

THESE SCANDALOUS STREETS I, II, III

FEAR MY GANGSTA I, II, III

THESE STREETS DON'T LOVE NOBODY I, II

BURY ME A G I, II, III, IV, V

**Tranay Adams**

THE STREETS ARE CALLING

**Duquie Wilson**

MARRIED TO A BOSS...

**By Destiny Skai & Chris Green**

Tranay Adams

## <u>KINGS OF THE GAME II</u>

**Playa Ray**

## **BOOKS BY LDP'S CEO, CA$H**

TRUST IN NO MAN

TRUST IN NO MAN 2

TRUST IN NO MAN 3

BONDED BY BLOOD

SHORTY GOT A THUG

THUGS CRY

THUGS CRY 2

THUGS CRY 3

TRUST NO BITCH

TRUST NO BITCH 2

TRUST NO BITCH 3

TIL MY CASKET DROPS

RESTRAINING ORDER

RESTRAINING ORDER 2

IN LOVE WITH A CONVICT

**Coming Soon**

BONDED BY BLOOD 2

BOW DOWN TO MY GANGSTA